For Kate Jone[illegible]

With Deep Affection

Ever Since Naples

And with love,

Penny [illegible]

THE CADILLAC OF SIX-BY'S

THE CADILLAC OF SIX-BY'S

REVERGE ANSELMO

HarperCollins*Publishers*

For information address HarperCollins*Publishers*,
10 East 53rd Street, New York, N.Y. 10022-5299.

HarperCollins books may be purchased for educational, business, or sales promotional use. For information, please write: Special Markets Department, HarperCollins*Publishers*,
10 East 53rd Street, New York, N.Y. 10022-5299.

First Edition

Designed by Anthony Ramondo

Library of Congress Cataloging-in-Publication Data

Anselmo, Reverge, 1962-
The Cadillac of six-by's / by Reverge Anselmo. — 1st ed.
p. cm.
ISBN 0-06-101209-2 (hardcover)
I. Title
PS3551.N7142C33 1997
813'.54—dc21 96-37380
CIP

---

97 98 99 00 ❖/HC 10 9 8 7 6 5 4 3 2 1

Historical Perimeter

IN THIS period of the Cold War, U.S. Pershing missiles were sent to western Europe to face down Soviet SS-20's in eastern Europe. Soviet troops were fighting in Afghanistan. Andropov ruled in Moscow. President Reagan increased strategic defenses for the United States. Soviet clients Iraq and Syria were fighting separate wars in the Near East. In 1982, Lebanon was a refuge for the PLO and other militant factions due to the instability brought on by years of civil war. In the spring of that year, Israeli forces invaded Lebanon. That summer, President Reagan sent U.S. Marines to evacuate besieged PLO fighters; the Marines left after completing the mission.

Soon thereafter, a car bomb killed the Lebanese president-elect, Bashir Gemayel, and gunmen went into the Palestinian refugee camps of Sabra and Shatila and massacred some seven hundred civilians. Twelve hundred Marines were sent back in-country as part of a multinational force to fill the vacuum left by the ousted PLO fighters, and they took up positions around Beirut International Airport. The presence of the multinational forces quieted Beirut initially, but as the months passed, factional fighting intensified in the city, the U.S. Embassy was bombed, multinational forces were attacked.

By the summer of 1983, Marines were being hit by artillery and rocket fire. The Marines then became engaged in entrenched line combat, being supported by artillery, and air and Naval gunfire. The chances of a Marine being killed in Beirut were, mathematically, one in five. On Sunday, October 23, 1983, suicide bombers attacked U.S. and French positions. The headquarters of First Battalion, Eighth Marine Regiment was destroyed, killing 241 men and one unidentified woman. The Marines were withdrawn from their positions in Lebanon in the spring of 1984.

What follows is a story born inside the closing wires of this forgotten scene.

Come from Lebanon, my bride, come from Lebanon, Come!

Descend from the top of Amana, from the top of Sanir and Hermon, from the haunts of the lions, from the leopard's mountains. You have ravished my heart, my sister, my bride; you have ravished my heart with one glance of your eyes, with one bead of your necklace. How beautiful is your love, my sister, my bride, how much more delightful is your love than wine, and the fragrance of your ointments than all spices! Your lips drip honey, my bride, and sweet meats and milk are under your tongue; and the fragrance of your garments is the fragrance of Lebanon.

The Song of Songs, IV, 8–11

THE CADILLAC OF SIX-BY'S

Pax Tecum Philomena

I

While in Search of a Dream

CLOUDS STACKED UP on the ocean side of the mountains in the afternoon and the range was hit with a purple broodlight like the color of the sea lying out beyond the city, where the Navy ships were driving in the water. The weather paraded with an Oriental drama, the loaded clouds and bursts of golding light spraying from the open bays of the sky. A blade of cloud-dark moved upon the range following the rolls and ravines ineffably. It spread like a robe over the ground, and still the sun lay out on the sea behind the ships and it struck into the gorges and gave shimmer to the range to the north. Pelicans looped in the air.

The patrol had turned and put its back to the ridgeline, which was pointed with great cedars and the pebbled walls of the villages there. They were breathing hard and cleansed by sweat. The sweat rolled the clinging city grit into black worms in folds of the skin. They had turned at the appointed steeps, and now they faced the crumbled city and the ocean and they were moving down now into it and into the gloom of the squall, which was pushing in the clammy taint of the shore and the fuming stench of the downtown grids.

From the last sloping heights the city fanned out, touching the water, giving off smoke, and sending up the rumble of traffic, rotor beats, and jet roars from the flat crossed runways surrounded by the rubbles of the squatting camps and the coast of the sea.

The patrol moved down a narrow road in a staggered column, passing the mutilated squat buildings, shot out and scorched, hung with banners of the Ayatollah, in a part of the city called the Hooterville. The road was pressed with women in purdah, rubble, racing children, vendors' carts, and little fires.

Cazetti heard artillery hitting up the range. Rushes of wind carried the concussions and a few autumn leaves, and fluttered the rifle slings and the dangling chinstraps in the column. The helmets ahead were loping. The radios hissed, the whip antennas went poinging along. The patrol had come into the snorting, careless, plowing tread that made Cazetti feel all right. It was, once again, that day, in that particular year, the Marine Corps' birthday. When the patrol came in they could all get drunk, and then Cazetti could go along to jail. He felt all right about it. It was a cheerful thought in the rain-charged gloom. A Naval jail had no uphill walking. There were no humps in the brig. He decided to accept the brig, if it were offered.

The grunt voices were calling out, "Rawhide! Rawhide! . . . Yah!"

They crossed the Sidon road and came into the olive groves near the perimeter where a pretty, black-eyed peasant girl with a blue and red rag on her head was walking between the trees. Cazetti stopped short and shot her picture with the long-range recon camera he was carrying. He shouldered it and aimed it as a rifle would have targeted her face. She slapped her face with her hands, and made a leap behind an olive tree, then peeked. Cazetti moved along.

The colonel's jeep, with two little red flags and eagle rank insignia, was driving on them from behind. The colonel was squinting at the line of rain ahead. His driver, Neale, was squinting too, at the colonel and at the road, and at the column of the men.

In the center of the column, Doc Latour turned

around. He had a large, cheese-appreciator's nose and wore his helmet cover flapping from his helmet at the back, which was a thing he liked, to immitate the Arabs. He began shouting a thing he liked to shout.

"Ve-hicle! From the rear!"

The platoon answered this way: "HUH!"

"Ve-hicle! From the rear!"

"HUH!"

Lieutenant Irish stopped him. "That's enough, Doc."

Then Doc Latour sang a thing he liked, with a fake old-hillbilly voice: "How many roads must a man walk down, before you call him a turtle?"

Some in the column started to stumble, enjoying a reason to laugh and get easy, and the lieutenant too, in his Russian-poet round glasses, stumbled. When the jeep came along the side, the colonel's face was stern, but pleased.

Neale leaned out of the jeep to tag Cazetti. The squinting folds of his cheek wrinkled to his jaws. "Your looey's looking for you. He's calling on the net. They put you up on charges."

Cazetti said, "Oh well. I know."

The jeep went creeping forward. The column looked sweaty, and on-hard grunty, footsore, dusty, fire-power packed, which is what the colonel liked. The colonel held the windshield and stood up, shouting in cadence: "Happy-birthday-gentlemen!"

The platoon returned it to him. "Happy-birthday-colonel-sir!"

The colonel dropped down in his seat again and Neale jerked the jeep away into the perimeter and disappeared behind the berms.

The road was straight and it pointed at checkpoint 76, with the bunkers looking gloomy in the gloomy light with sand dunes, the runways and the sea beyond, the rain line coming over the water. The column reached the checkpoint, each man holding his balls and grunting, and shouting "Holy war!" There was a sign there on the bunker, a placard painted white-on-black in freehand letters:

USMC
POSITIONS FOUNDED
IN NOVEMBER 1982
WHILE IN SEARCH OF A DREAM

A Marine on post stuck his head out of the bunker. "That's one for the Navy, gents!"

When Doc Latour crossed inside the perimeter he leaned on his knees and looked out his helmet side at Corporal Paugh and the line of incoming men.

There was a Lebanese soldier at the checkpoint looking on. The Doc reeled over his side and landed on his back, on his pack looking up with his legs kicked to his chest. He moaned and twisted around to scratch himself in his gear.

Corporal Paugh got sore. "You *are* a squid, Doc. You turtleback. You suck. You slime around. You embarrass me in front of the Lebs, and you're a squid-squiddly-bungdoctor." Corporal Paugh began to stomp back through the line of the patrol as they passed the bunker. His face was large and hard boned, and dirt stuck to stubble on his lip and chin. He was what the colonel liked to see in a field Marine.

"Any man in my squad who turtlebacks at the perimeter gets his ass kicked in, and gets no booze, and goes on watch. Bungdoctor! Get up!"

The Doc got up. "Oh, Corporal Paugh is scary. He's so gruesome. He's so cruel. I wish he was my friend."

"Doc, slide along and shut up, huh?" Paugh stomped off.

On the perimeter road, the canopied deuce-and-a-half trucks called Six-by's were rolling up loaded with men from the line companies set in at the south. The rain came.

Lieutenant Irish stopped with the radioman who stood there blank eyed like a horse. The lieutenant's glasses got pebbled by raindrops. He keyed on the handset and got a tone burst: "Valuable—Valuable, be advised. Bravo Comp'ny Second Platoon is back in poz at this time." While the radio talk went on, the lieutenant started waving in Cazetti and Corporal Paugh at double-time and directing their eyes to the figure of the company commander who was standing in the distance at the Command Post. At the last tone burst the lieutenant sent the radioman ahead and said: "Paugh, take the men in and draw the chow. And turn the comp'ny commander's back so he don't see Cazetti. Cazetti: Turn away from the comp'ny commander." Lieutenant Irish turned Cazetti by the shoulders. "Don't let him see you with my platoon. Catch one of those Six-by's and go home. And listen up, if you can, see about getting some of that hard booze up at the COC for us tonight."

"Oh, dig it, sir," Paugh said.

"Roger to that, sir. No sweat. There's a lot of Johnny Walker up there. Later-on, sir. Later-on, Paugh. Tell Doc I said later-on."

Cazetti ran down the perimeter road to get a Six-by. The rain beat, making it muddy and pooling the rivulets. The Marines on post put their rain gear on. It made them look like metal manatees. A couple of two-rotor choppers were whipping off the runways to go out to the ships offshore. The rain hit on the tarmac and the helo rotors spun it in a darkened vortex.

A Six-by was coming with a driver Cazetti knew. It was a Motor-T sergeant with an undershot jaw and a carefully blocked soft-cover on his head, named Yoches. Cazetti waved and the Six-by stopped.

"Yoches, You got any room in that Six-by?"

"Don't ask, Cazetti. You know better than that. My old Six-by's just like a foxhole . . . always room for one more."

Cazetti kicked up into the back of the truck filled with Charlie Company grunts, and he rode standing, holding on to the rim of the canvas. He saw a white burro, with a sagging belly and furry jaws, tied to a leafless olive tree near the perimeter wire, and a yellow building pocked with bullet holes that had a machine-gun crew on the top of it who were trying to break a rectangular block of ice in half with the serrated edge of an entrenching tool.

Motorized flatbeds on wheels, called Mules, kept buzzing on the road in both directions faster than the Six-by's moved. The canvas on the campaign tents sagged in the rain, making the post centers look nipple-like. An amphibious assault vehicle was parked with its beveled aquatic prow facing the sea, the barrel of the .50-caliber pointed down in a droop. A grumbling M-60 tank was traveling backwards and the tank commander, standing in the cupola, stuck his finger in his ear. Sandbag walls around the hooches and bunkers had transistor radios resting on them, playing the U.S. Armed Forces channel, and everything inside the perimeter felt homey.

There was a lot of gear shuffling, and unloading, and men milling around at the headquarters where Cazetti dropped off of the truck. The place was a square of bullet-spattered, half-blown buildings between the two arms of the runways. The runways were surrounded by the Hooterville and the sea. Between the buildings were a jeep park and a line of plane trees. There were campaign tents on either side of the jeep park. These touched either end of the one-story building with six ribbed-iron garage doors that accounted for the Combat Operations Center for the U.S. Forces Ashore.

All the drivers were sitting in rain gear on the hoods of the jeeps, or inside them under their tarpaulin tops, making jokes and lighting up cigarettes with Zippos. The driving crew was, as ever, waiting for the officers to make a run to somewhere out to the lines, or the city, or the hills. Cazetti wanted to sit with them.

Neale tugged him by the buckle of his war-belt. "Man, you better go see your looey. Some line-company officer put you on charges."

So Cazetti turned and walked into the building, and he passed the sergeant-major who had a pirate's voice, and tangs of flesh that hung off the corners of his mouth. The sergeant-major put a finger hard on Cazetti's throat, and said, "You goddamn make me sick. All you Intell pukes, you make me sick. You think you're smart? You give me zits. Take those goddamn gloves out of your war-belt, and uncover your head when you walk into my COC. Do you roger?" Cazetti looked at the sergeant-major without saying anything. "You goddamn make me sick, I said," repeated the sergeant-major. "And you're going to the brig."

With the sergeant-major's finger still stuck to his throat, Cazetti rotated past him, lifting his helmet, and slipped into the COC.

In the rainy days the bare hanging bulbs cast a peculiar yellow light inside the room, which was crammed with radios and radiomen, and movement and messaging. Field phones rang in all corners. The walls were covered with maps. Officers scratched under the straps of their shoulder holsters. An oil heating stove of Lebanese design had canteen cups and C-rat cans on it, sending steam and food smell into the air, which was damp.

The intelligence section was screened off from the rest of the COC by a wall of stacked-up mount-out boxes. At the entrance signs were hung:

S-2

WHAT WE DON'T KNOW WILL HURT YOU.

Another sign showed two spy characters drawing guns on each other and the words:

WHO KNOWS WHAT EVIL LURKS IN THE HEARTS OF MEN?
THE -2 DO

Intell pukes had a habit of mumbling in fantoned voices with their faces close together. Lieutenant Cercio sat at his desk and Davey and Garces leaned across it. The lieutenant's face had a prep school in it, but it was an athletic prep school that had left him with a solid chin. Davey had a face as flat and as white as a cracker, with grape-green eyes that never blinked. He turned the unblinking eyes to Cazetti.

"Hey, bud."

"Davey," Cazetti said. He inclined his head to Garces. "Lord Garces."

"Don't effect a nonchalance, Cazetti," Garces said.

"Davey nonchalanced, so I nonchalanced."

"Secure from this," said the lieutenant.

Garces had a lot of hair on his head for a Marine. It was black and he used pomade on it. He liked to keep up an aristocratic toilette, even in the field. He stood up while Lieutenant Cercio squeezed his eyes at the bridge of his nose, and folded his arms on the desk.

"You just want to embarrass your lieutenant. Is that it, Cazetti?" Garces said. "You decided to mortify the whole intelligence community, so that we are all shamed on your account. That's your plan. Right? To make us look ridiculous? Is this your aim? Is it your aim in life?"

Cazetti sagged, dropped his field gear to the floor and unslung his rifle and recon camera, laying the camera in a gentle way on the desk.

Lieutenant Cercio spoke with a hoarse Boston accent. "I have a charge sheet here. From Bravo Comp'ny commander, Captain Turling. Here."

He handed the charge sheet to Garces. "Read it to him."

Garces read it. "'Soliciting sexual commerce from female Hooterville Hey-Joe across perimeter fence.' The language is very strong and specific, and I'm pleased to say you're going to burn."

"Now, is this true?" Lieutenant Cercio asked.

"No, sir," Cazetti said. "We touched tongues."

"What?" Davey asked.

"I touched her tongue with my tongue."

"Why?" Davey asked.

"She suggested it. She said, 'Let's touch tongues.'"

"Like that? 'Let's touch tongues.' . . . Was she Moslem?" Lieutenant Cercio asked.

"Yes, sir. From Hooterville. She wasn't good-looking or anything. She was just there, wrapped in a rag. I think it's true, that part about her being a Hey-Joe. I felt sorry for her."

"And is that supposed to mitigate it?" Garces asked. "You are going to burn, Cazetti. No one can help you now. No one *should* help you now. Because you are a bad person. That is what you are. You're riddled with weakness and discontent, and a very bad karma is about you, is it not?"

Lieutenant Cercio said, "The tongue-touching

. . . was it a transaction that involved any money or goods?"

"No, sir. It was not."

"She didn't ask for money? She didn't ask for anything? Did you give her anything?"

"Just my tongue, sir."

"Why?" Davey asked again.

"It's a thing I believe about fate. 'Meet Cute.'"

Garces said, "Meet the courts-martial. That's what you should say. You're lucky you still have a tongue left, Cazetti. You don't know what a woman can do. A woman can make provisions on her insides with contraptions that can cut your dick up. Did you know that? That happened in Nam more than once."

"That; I don't know about that, Garces. Anyway, her tongue was outside. She put it through the fence. I could see it, before I touched it. It was a nice tongue."

"How long did the tongue-touching continue?" Lieutenant Cercio asked.

"Not long, sir. It was not sustained."

"Not sustained." The lieutenant wrote that down.

"No, sir. I talked to her a little while. She spoke French."

"Oh," Davey said. "She spoke French."

"Yes, she did. I was waiting for Second Platoon

to mount up for the foot patrol. Captain Turling just came along right at the . . . the . . . uh . . ."

"Touching of the tongues," the lieutenant supplied.

"Yes, sir."

Lieutenant Cercio looked at Davey and Garces for comment. They didn't have any. The lieutenant said, "This is for the colonel to decide. But you secure from this conduct, Cazetti. I'm serious. You're enlisted. Remember that."

"Okay, sir."

"What'd you see out there with Bravo, bud?" Davey asked.

"I'll show you."

Cazetti went to stand at the tactical maps on the wall and the others followed to look on. While they stood, the sergeant-major barked out an announcement: "Every swinging dick fall out in formation for the cutting of the cake at LZ Rock. Repeat: Every swinging dick." Some of the radiomen started to file out.

Cazetti began pointing at grids on the maps. "Five miles out there were lots of young men in civvies, more than you would usually see, riding in cars, and it looked like they were heading up the road to Alayah, or to Bhamdoun. PLO, Druze, I don't know. Israelis are all over . . . moving up the mountains with snow parkas and big equipment. Bulldozers, backhoes, semis."

"Okay, they're staying for the winter." Davey said.

"They got any skiing up there?" asked the lieutenant.

"I didn't see any snow. Maybe higher up. You ski, sir?"

"I love to ski."

"Yes, sir," Cazetti said. "We came back down through Ba'abda. I saw Gunner Minovich and Sergeant Cain with Joe Sfir at that Lebs-2 house, so you know that means the Joe Sfir end of the Phalange wants something from the Lebs-2. And I figure he wants this thing bad if he's going in there with our guys."

"Or else, he wants us to think he wants what he tells the Lebs he wants," Davey said.

"While really that wanker wants something completely different," Lieutenant Cercio said, "But Minovich will know. Have him brief me when he gets in."

"Right, sir," said Garces. "Very astute, sir. That analysis was very much an 'In the Root' way of thinking. I'm pleased to say, I'm learning from you, sir."

Lieutenant Cercio shook his fingers near his ears. "Lick not upon boot, Garces . . ."

"No, sir. No, sir," Garces said. "Right. Anything else, Cazetti? Anything atypical? Anything you sensed? Anything you photographed?"

Cazetti cast his arm out and hit the grid square with his thumb. "A nice-looking girl in the Hooterville olive grove. And I mean *nice.*"

"Excellent," the lieutenant said. "But don't talk to her. You're secured from that conduct. At least, where any grunt officer can see you."

"I know, sir."

"All right. Let's go get cake," Lieutenant Cercio said. Garces lingered to fold a laminated map. While the lieutenant and Davey walked out of the COC with Cazetti trailing, the lieutenant turned and said, "You know, you've got huge arms, Cazetti."

And Cazetti said, "I do? . . . Thanks, sir."

Outside the rain was pecking in a lighter way, fading to a drizzle. Elements for the ceremony of the birthday cake at LZ Rock were combining. Reporters climbed up aircraft maintenance scaffolds set around the tail of a cargo jet. Clutching the bars, they looked like corpses dangling from the scaffolds. The tail of the cargo jet was chewed up by bullet holes. The men fell in to dense formations in the shape of a bracket around a field desk covered with a tarp. The cake sat on it. They were waiting for the colonel to arrive. The Sixth Fleet band was playing "Stateside" and it echoed off the hangars and the hills, and all the helmets made a slinky on the heads of the guys who were enjoying it. Almaza beer trucks were standing by with the sides rolled up.

Neale brought the colonel in his jeep, and fell in with the driving crew where Cazetti was standing with Mangas, a copper-faced half Mexican, and a Bayonne Italian slob called Chick Cicchelero. When the colonel walked to the center the band began to play "Over the Waves."

A freak event took place. It was discreet but it was observed. A small brown bird swooped across the tarmac and landed on Cazetti, perching on the gloves that were looped over the buckle of his war-belt. It chirped, rubbed its head against his belly, chirped, rubbed its head again.

Neale whispered to Mangas with his teeth clenched, "Check out this thing, man. There's a bird on Cazetti." Mangas looked as far to the side as he could without moving his head.

The sergeant-major called for attention and the bird flew off toward the hills.

The colonel made a speech: "This is the day I thank God that I belong to the Marine Corps, and that all of you men here belong to me. We are in the Suck as one. I will toast this day, and you will toast it with me. And Lebanon will toast us all together. Let the oldest Marine piss with the youngest Marine, and let us thank God for three things: In the first place, we are men. In the second place, we are Marines. In the third place, we are field Marines."

Great cheers and grunting swelled as the colonel cut the cake. Harmonicas and horns rang out from the band. The beer trucks were pillaged. In this way the feast began, and certain elements lingered on the tarmac while others drifted back to the tents and roofs, the bars and vehicles in pools of drinking conspiracies, or they went on watch and conspired later.

Wind blew into the palms and plane trees, dancing them, carrying the smoky damp and songs around the compound. At the time when the headquarters area was a crash of music and drinking, Cazetti saw Gunner Minovich and Sergeant Cain return from their journeys with Joe Sfir. They walked into the COC. They picked up coffee in their canteen cups from a coffee bull and sipped it, walking, moving back to the Intell section where Lieutenant Cercio was seated, with Davey and Garces and Cazetti in a circle around him. The lieutenant was pouring scotch into improvised tumblers.

"Here come the gods," Garces said. He slanted an eyebrow for the benefit of Minovich.

"The what?" asked the lieutenant.

"A term of praise, sir," Garces said.

"Don't praise anymore, Garces."

"No, don't," Minovich said. "If you do, I'll take a peach can and put it on the stove until it's hot, and then I'll press it into your forehead until you have a nice red ring on your head. You want to be called Ring Head?"

Davey burst out laughing, which was rare. Garces smiled and looked around.

Minovich was lean, and ruddy faced. The back of his neck was freckled, and blond hair curled up out of the collar of his blouse to the base of his ears. He wore aviator's glasses and a shoulder-holstered pistol as well as an AK-47 on his shoulder. His bottom lip was bulged with Skoal. He squatted down to stretch.

"I only intended to convey respect," Garces said.

"It's flattery. Secure from it."

"Yes, sir. I see. The remark was off the mark. But well intended, I promise you, sir."

Cain lifted Cazetti's peach can full of scotch

from the desk, and whispered over his shoulder, "Garces, do slurpy, do licky?" He poured some scotch into his coffee.

Cazetti said, "Roger to that," and pointed at the spot on the desk where the peach can belonged, in front of him, and Cain reset it. Cain had a big green automatic shotgun on his back. He started to unsling it. The sling grew taut and scraped him as it spread the slant of his shoulders and neck and head. He was formed of heavy packs of meat and paws. His back was thick as a field desk.

"Gunner Minovich. First of all, happy birthday," Lieutenant Cercio said, offering him the bottle.

"Happy birthday, Lieutenant." Minovich waved the bottle under his nose and drank straight from the neck.

"Cazetti says he saw you in Ba'abda with Joe Sfir. Is that right?"

"Just so," said Minovich.

"Was the Hitman there?"

"No. He took Joe's car up to the mountains."

"What's Joe Sfir want from the Lebs-2?"

"His story was, he had intelligence for trade. X for Y . . . if they'd cooperate. They wouldn't. The Lebs didn't like it. They're getting stuck-up about dealing with the Phalange."

"Snooty. For real," Cain said.

Davey asked, "Was the trade for the Phalange? Or just private—for Joe Sfir, entrepreneur?"

"Both," Cain said.

"He's got guns he wants to sell," said Minovich. "And dope. And he wasn't the last man to notice that the new Leb army is a bigger market than the Phalange was going to be."

"The profit motive," the lieutenant said. "That's sincere, I guess, you think?"

"With Joe Sfir . . . yes, sir," said Minovich. "Let's say, I'm Joe Sfir; a Christian Leb. I say, I got a neutral army between me and my enemy. Okay, this *army,* the U.S. holds it up, makes it bigger than my own militia: I want to work with this *army,* I want contacts, I want inroads, I want to deal. I go and pay a visit to this *army,* with my *friends* from the Marine Corps."

"Still," Lieutenant Cercio said. "I don't like Joe. Why can't I get over that? I like his women, but I don't like him. . . . Cazetti saw gooners in mufti heading up to Bhamdoun and Alayah. Did Joe know about that?"

"He knew, sir," Cain said. "And he knew Lebs-2 would say they didn't know. But they knew too. It's why Hitman went to the mountains."

The sergeant-major's bar for the enlisted men glowed with candlelights speared by shouldered rifles from the crowd of men. The brass horns from the Sixth Fleet band and the whistling cheers from the Battalion below vibrated in the bar with the talk going on inside it. The unit emblem, a giant mushroom cloud with a bolt of lightning jumping through it, was painted on the back wall behind the counter.

"It was the evil eye. He's a narc. I swear to God," Cicchelero said.

"What kind of a narc is in the Suck?" Neale asked.

"I dunno. Some kind of a narc."

Mangas said, "Who's the guy gonna narc on? Us? Other jarheads?"

"Maybe he ain't a real jarhead. See?" said Cicchelero.

Neale said, "Oh. You think that bald head and field gear, and humping around the Root is a disguise? I mean, come on man, what kind of a narc?"

"I dunno, some narcs, you never know. But he works for Intell and he's some kind of a narc, okay?"

"Doggone. You're a real bright guy," Mangas said. "What'd you say your name was?"

"Chick. Cicchelero."

"I know that. I mean your first name."

"Tony. Does that stun you?"

"Listen, Tony. That's a pal of mine you're talking about. You eat too much food. You mind if I say it?"

"What food do I eat?"

"Piles and tons, man," Neale said.

"Yo, shut up," Cicchelero said. "Check it out: At sea, when we were passing Sicily, and that's where I'm from, so respect it, Cazetti brings up classified traffic to the colonel. Pretty soon he sits down. Yo. He don't come out for an hour and a half. Now, what was the colonel and the corporal talking about for an hour and a half? He's a narc."

"You need something dietetic, my friend," said Mangas. He looked at Cicchelero hard and took his beer can from him. "Very dietetic."

"Colonel likes the guy. That's all. Give me a smoke," Neale said. Mangas gave him one. When he dragged on it, Neale's jaws, which were always pulsing, made a sound like a click from his throat. "I don't know if I like that tattoo he's got though; big old horse pistol, and the thing says 'Honey You Lied.' Who lied? You know?"

"He shot some babe he was married to or

something. It's in his file. A judge sent him to the Suck. But that bird comes back for revenge. *Malocchio.*"

"That could be true, man," Neale said. "Mangas, you think that's possible?"

"No. I know the guy. He's a horn-dog, motorized. But no wife."

"That's what I mean. He's a get-laid kind of a guy, and she did something, or she didn't do something, and he put her in the ground. Yo, give my beer back."

"No," Mangas said. "I'll put it in the ground." He poured the beer on the floor and looked at Neale.

"That's low, but I don't give," Cicchelero said. "You guys know Cossaboom? He keeps the files in the brig on ship."

"Oh, man!" Neale said, "The sweaty albino guy with the Bible in his hand . . . what a freak! Yeah, I know him."

"Cossaboom says when you do this numberology thing . . ." Cicchelero looked left and right along the bar. "Yo. Listen: Cazetti equals Luciifer, with one extra 'i' somewhere."

Mangas said, "My friend, you do stun me. Doggone."

Cicchelero waved his hand at his cheek. "But then it really gets spooky. Cossaboom says the devil can appear like an angel. And he speaks foreign languages. And *Cazetti,* good-looking guy, right? He speaks French, but he's Italian? Huh? from Pomona, New York? And he ain't a narc? Listen up: He's *possessed,* according to Cossaboom. Yo. He punched out Cossaboom when Cossaboom was reading *Revelations* out loud."

"Is that what Cossaboom said?" asked Neale. "That's scary. The two of you together, that's frightening. He's your only friend, I hope."

Mangas said, "He didn't punch him out. He *pinched* him."

"No way," said Cicchelero.

"He pinched him."

"Okay. Yo. *Why?"*

"Because Cossaboom wouldn't shut up. And then he did shut up."

"Still, foreign languages, and that."

Neale said, "Check it out with Cossaboom. He keeps the records on the ship. The Suck sent him to language school in Monterey. It's in his file. So just relax, Chick."

They saw Cazetti walk into the bar then, holding something heavy which was dangling in a sandbag. He spoke to Cicchelero and pinched the back of his arm. "You know where Bravo is?"

"Uh, yeah."

"Second Platoon's in front of the mortars. Take this down to Corporal Paugh. Or a lieutenant in glasses named Irish. I know how many bottles are in here and I'll find out if they go UA. I'll give you ten bucks. So do it. Okay?"

"Okay," Cicchelero said. He took the bag and drove out in a jeep.

It was night. Flashes of artillery struck the range. On the road before the compound, the motors from two idling Six-by's covered down the sounds of the Battalion beer party. Drizzle blew across the headlights. Battery grunts were climbing into them with beer cans in their hands, and cigarettes began to glow in the caves of the truck.

"Don't get separated from Neale," the colonel said. He was an extremely large and ugly man with book-leather skin. He spoke to Mangas who sat at the wheel of his jeep. "The run goes to Alayah, to the Phalange hospital. Radio up if the Six-by's lag. Who's your shotgun?"

"It's Cazetti, sir," said Cazetti from the outboard seat.

"Lock and load as soon as we get out of here. . . . You been drinking?"

"Yes, sir."

"Good enough. Let's go."

"I like that guy," Mangas said.

The convoy pulled out, smashing the puddles, pressing through checkpoints up the airport road with rain falling and the city ahead glowing under the clouds in an awful orange mist light. They passed the minaret tower of the blown mosque, lit from its base by a fire in a drum. Arc lights at the Italian camp made their fence wires look black against the glare. The jeeps turned right at Shatila camp to head over the Green Line. All the buildings were torn and bullet-pocked, dark within, or dim-lit. Rubble spilled into the road showed in the headlights and the convoy jolted over stones. Soon they were grinding up roads, getting always narrower and steeper, in the looming dark uphill.

The convoy pulled up to a yard in front of a great yellow stone building with the red cross in a white field painted over the wide entry doors which were topped by a balcony. A band in white uniforms with blue garrison hats stood on it at attention with their instruments under their arms. The whine of the Six-by motors slowed and chortled. Floodlights illuminated from the balustrade along the roof.

"Look at this," Cazetti said.

Mangas bent his neck and leaned his head to look up from under his helmet through the windshield. "Unreal."

Flowers stuck in rolls of leafy garland scalloped the facade. There were rows of patients sitting robed in wheelchairs with umbrellas, waiting before the doors, men and women. Among the women, two stood out in particular, strangely draped, with their backs to a little herd of Nubian goats. One stood erect and had an aged face recessed into the funnel of a great gray woolen cowl of a long robe. The other, beside her, wore a cowl mantled over her shoulders in a rich kind of way. The crisp white mantilla on her head gleamed in the floodlight gaily from the dark, and her head was crowned with a sort of white pillbox toque with a blue cross stitched in the center.

Both women had crucifixes on chains around their necks. The younger woman moved her hands to the crucifix. There was a pouch on the front of her gray robe. She inserted the stem of the crucifix into this pouch, and carried it like a joey kangaroo. Cazetti took these two for supervisors from some elaborate nursing corps.

The battery grunts unloaded from the trucks while the calls for formation were barked by the sergeants. The colonel made ceremonial handshakes with the hospital staff. The band struck the "Battle Hymn of the Republic."

Mangas and Cazetti got out of the jeep. Cazetti unlocked his rifle, looked into the chamber, and reseated the magazine in its pouch. The formation was dismissed and a swirl of greeting and excitement developed between the patients and the battery grunts. Cazetti and Mangas moved to the side of the crowd with Neale to get into the building.

"We hit the big hickey now, man," Neale said. The crowd began moving in.

The young nurse had her hands on the back of a paralytic's chair. Her hands kept flying from the handles and shaking with the fingertips stiff, as though they had a magnetic current ruling them. Her nose tended to go pointing around when she spoke to her older colleague or the man in the chair. She was evidently delighted.

As they came in with the crowd, shuffling through the doorway, Cazetti got stuck waiting behind the young nurse who was pushing the paralytic man. Cazetti had his eyes locked onto the back of her head, and he was seized with an impulse to put his nose near the cloth of the white mantilla and the asprin-shaped toque, which seemed certain to offer a pretty fragrance.

He did not. Mangas and Neale were already ahead in the bright-lit interior.

"Welcome! Hello! American! *Alahn wa Salahn!*"

The hall inside was a swirl of movement and clamor and yellow brightness from the chandeliers over great tables set with linen, goblets, silver, and flowers. There were glass carafes of wine on the tables as well as pitchers of water and floating ice cubes, and on platters there were whole bottles of spirits and treats.

Mangas pulled Cazetti down at a table where he was sitting with Neale and a dark-haired young boy. The young nurse put her paralytic next to Cazetti.

"I *intro-duece,* Kalil," she said. Her nose twittered. She had moist brown eyes which conveyed a cheery and simple regard. The fine skin under her eyes was darker, and a faint delicate smudge touched her eyes with a declining, tender quality. She made a little gasp and spun away to fetch a toddling boy in short pants who had put his feet into a helmet and was rocking in it.

Cazetti reached to shake hands with Kalil, but noticed it was not possible, because the man's palsy had knotted his hand and made it useless.

"Big hickey in the big-time way," Neale said. He was pouring out the wine. "Man, no doubt."

"Do you guys speak English?" Mangas asked the dark-haired boy.

"Kalil does not speak it," said the boy. The band began to play waltzes, and the boy had to raise his voice. "I am Pierre," he said. "I was hit in my back at the time of Begin and the jets."

"Are you going to walk again?" Mangas asked him.

"I don't know. Kalil is not. He has damage in the spine and brain."

"You're a very frank guy," Mangas said, while Neale and Cazetti looked across at each other, tensed.

"Yes," said Pierre.

Cazetti helped Kalil by putting a glass filled with wine to his lips. Kalil smiled a little. Cazetti had rested a cigarette in the ashtray, and Kalil made a plea for one of his own with his eyes and a slant of the head. Neale reached across to light it for him after Cazetti stuck it in his mouth. They all lit up. Food came around steaming on trays carried by nurses in white smocks and waiters wearing black vests.

"Do you like the Phalange?" Pierre asked Neale.

"Is that what you are?"

"Of course."

"Then I like the Phalange. It's a good name, man, and you've got class."

"Do you know what is our cause? This display is to win you to our cause."

"No," Mangas said. "What's that?"

"That we control the Lebanon. The others are all tribes of communist barbarians."

"Well, our creed," Cazetti said, "is kill a commie for mommy, wherever you can find one."

"Yes? A good creed," Pierre said.

"Besides that, we have no politics. We just sit on ships and wait to go in somewhere. Somewhere with Bravo. Somewhere where there's communists. Neale hates communists."

"What about the Moslem?" asked Pierre.

"Well, I hate those because I'm a Catholic. Neale doesn't mind them. He's a Protestant."

"Wait up, man," Neale said, "I do mind them. I hate them too."

"You? Get serious."

"I'm with Cazetti," Mangas said. "How can a Protestant guy hate Moslems, Pierre? You know what I mean?"

"Just by doing it," Neale said.

"Let me tell you something, Neale. Us Catholic guys crusaded. We came down these mountains again and again, hitting the Saladin in Palestine. You people stayed up in, in—I don't know—Nordic places, making cheese roundels. You're Boots to the Root."

Mangas, with enthusiasm and assent, was nodding his head.

"That's so messed up, Cazetti," Neale said. "Man, we crusaded. I crusaded. Everyone was Catholic in the Crusades. There wasn't any Protestants till later. So don't call me a Boot. I can hate a Moslem just as good as you."

"He's correct," said Pierre.

"Oh," Cazetti said. "I didn't know that. I apologize."

Mangas said, "Now what do we do?"

"I know," Cazetti said. "Pierre, what's the name of the nurse who brought Kalil to the table?"

"There was no nurse."

"Yeah there was. She had a white thing on her head, and she was cute."

"She was not a nurse. She was a nun."

Cazetti was angry. "What?"

"What kind of a Catholic are you?" Neale asked.

"I'm the kind you find. I'm lapsed, all right? And I don't care. I want to know her name. Tell me this nun's name."

"Her name is Philomena," said Pierre.

"Oh, that figures," Cazetti said. "A nun name. And a nun. What a load. Damn it."

"What you're thinking," Mangas said, pointing at Cazetti's eye, "you just don't think it."

Unit insignia, captured relics, badges, jump wings, berets, and pins came around the tables being traded. Soft-covers and metal collar chevrons were stripped while the drinking carried on.

The waltzes were over and there was chatter droning from the tables in the hall for a while. Flags were coming off the balcony for souvenirs, and then the Hitman came in from the kitchen doors with an AK-47 on his back. He walked to the colonel's table slowly while looking around, made the gesture of a couple of bows to the colonel and the hosts. He folded his hands behind his back. He then crouched next to the colonel and spoke to him.

Cazetti saw him come in and said, "Neale," and he jerked his head and said, "Hitman," and Neale looked.

"Where?" Neale said.

"With the colonel."

"I don't see him."

"He dropped down."

"Where is he?"

"You'll see him in a second."

"Did he carry in the AK?"

"Yeah."

"There he is," Neale said. "I thought he had white hair. And I thought he always walked around with a bulldog."

Cazetti had to drop some ashes for Kalil, and lift up for him a drink of wine.

"Who told you that?" Cazetti said.

"Cossaboom."

Cazetti laughed.

Neale tweaked Mangas's sleeve to turn his head from Pierre. "The cat-eye dude with the high forehead standing next to the colonel. AK. That's Hitman. They say he's got something lurking in his heart."

"I guess he does," Mangas said.

The band on the balcony was carefully swelling and the chatter and clink at table began to fall off. Then it was still enough to hear the bells on the goats float in and mingle with the gentle circling scales. Cazetti felt a chill. Philomena appeared on the balcony. She closed her eyes to concentrate. There was a crease between her eyebrows. She made all her fingernails touch and her hands were still on her breast. Her nose went pointing a little. She kept her eyes closed, she licked the ledge of her lips, and she was singing the "Ave Maria."

The song was solemn and lilting. Faces winced from the way it pierced. It resonated anciently. It cast a stupefying beauty in the glowing room, in the sparkle of the chandeliers. Cazetti needed something to hold. He was afraid to breathe because he felt he would cry if he did. He grabbed the clubbed hand of Kalil, and started crying.

They filed out later with the flags in a stream, the berets being twirled in the floodlights. The battery grunts went into the trucks and the jeeps led them down from the mountain. It was quiet. Mangas lit two cigarettes. His face glowed red from the lighter under the helmet, and from the dashboard gauges. He handed one of the cigarettes to Cazetti.

"Don't talk. Okay?" Cazetti said. He smoked and looked out at the firelights and the city. He wanted to be by himself.

The convoy got back to the headquarters at midnight and there was still a candle glow in the enlisted bar, where a half dozen leaners with cans of beer in their hands were singing "American Pie." Cazetti wanted to go to his cot to wrap his head up tight in a poncho liner in the dark so he could remember the singing and the pretty details of the charming nun without talking to anyone.

He moped along the front of the COC where Davey was leaning his gut against the sandbag wall talking to Minovich. They were talking about Khe-Sahn, and hill 881, details that Davey had seen from the ground, views that Minovich remembered from the air, when he had been a crew chief on a Huey. The colonel was walking into the building and they stiffened, saluted him, and leaned on the wall again. Minovich screwed the tin medallion off his canister of Skoal and offered Davey a dip. They both dipped. When Cazetti came along, they stopped Cazetti and pulled him back toward the jeep park by the war-belt.

"Listen, bud. You got a mission. Tonight." Davey sucked through his teeth and spat on the ground.

"Oh, come on. No. I feel tired and I can't do a mission. I just did one." Cazetti leaned back against the hood of a jeep.

Minovich spat on the ground. "I feel you can. I feel you listening, and doing, and obeying, and accomplishing. I feel all of that."

"You got to go get the lieutenant," Davey said.

"Where is he?"

"He's stuck downtown. One of Joe Sfir's girls has got an apartment at the University, up behind the Embassy."

"Who's going with me?"

"Nobody," Minovich said. "That's the beauty of it. Nobody is to go, and nobody is to know. Nobody ever went, and the lieutenant was never where he's at. And so, Cazetti, we thought of you, naturally. We imagined Cazetti not doing what he was never told to do. Am I clear?"

"Where's this apartment?"

"You just show up at the Embassy at exactly zero-two. The lieutenant meets you there. Take my pistol," Davey said. He took his holster off his shoulder. "Aim high, hit low."

They separated. Cazetti had to kill time so he went into the enlisted bar. He was sore, and aggravated. He got a beer and lit a cigarette in the flame of a candle and sat down on sandbags with Mangas, scowling in the wavering shadow. Cicchelero was hunched at the bar next to a lanky Alabama redneck with big teeth who was called Yuck.

Neale was talking with a midget sniper called Ballory. Neale got excited whenever he discovered other Marines from Minnesota. He liked to name high schools and hear they'd been heard of. He liked to name lakes and hear they'd been fished. He had a passion for Ski-Doo's, and so did Ballory.

"I thought you were hitting the rack," Mangas said.

"I'm staying up a while," Cazetti said.

"Where'd you get the .45?"

"Davey told me to clean it for him. How do you feel about Minnesota?"

"Well, I don't feel anything about it, to be honest."

"Do you feel like hearing about it?"

"I don't care. What's doggone with you?"

Cazetti swigged off his beer and stared at the emblem on the wall. Yuck turned around from the bar and thought Cazetti was looking at him.

"Neale," Cazetti said. "Can you and Ballory secure from that Minnesota butter talk? It's boring for the rest of us, you know."

"Ahre you gonna *cry* if he don't?" Yuck looked at Cazetti with his head slacked to his shoulder.

"Lighten up, man," Neale said.

"He's gonna *cry*, like a *narc.*"

"Who asked for a contribution from the Klan member?" Cazetti said. He stood up.

Yuck took his elbow off the bar. "You gonna

try the Klan, young man? You might get yo' goozler into trouble if you do."

Mangas took the pistol and the rifle off Cazetti's shoulder before he started to move towards Yuck. Cazetti didn't altogether notice he was doing that. He only stared straight at Yuck's face, and when he moved, his arms were cocked and his knuckles were swelled from his fist.

A wind had risen and it was raining again. The rain dragged from the low, moving clouds. The city was muffled in it. Going up the airport road, the wind beat the rain into the jeep from the shore side and Cazetti was getting soaked. He opened the heating baffles, and warm air blew onto his legs. It felt good. He conceived he was alone, even with the whole darkened city around him, which was dangerous, but it was a relief. He tried to think of the singing but he couldn't hum it or summon it at all. It was gone. His mind kept repeating the burst of beer vomit hitting Cicchelero's boots when he had beaten Yuck on the floor. He thought about charges, and the possible specifics, and he began rehearsing defenses for himself, imagining a sit-down with Lieutenant Cercio.

There was fog when he came up to the Sabra

camp. A black flag on a pole was flapping over the great mass grave under the arc lights of the Italian camp where the sick, sweet death smell rose from the ground of the massacre. There were no vehicles on the road, and the jeep flew past the circle around the Shatila camp, and went along down the wide, empty boulevard to town. He drove into Martyr Square which was dark, and ghostly, muddy, empty, and the motor sent a terrible lonely shock through the desolate square. The great old neon signs that crowned the buildings there were blown out and collapsed. Openings in the buildings were caught by the headlights which peered at the fathomless darkness within, and the rain running on the road was swirling around the chunks of rubble. There was a Lebanese checkpoint ahead where a lone yellow bulb glowed between two figures inside the narrow shelter. They waved at Cazetti's jeep, and Cazetti yelled out, *"Marhaba!"* and the two Lebanese shouted it back. The jeep twisted through another smashed, deserted area, and then the lights from the corniche appeared, and the U.S. Embassy appeared. It was lit up from within.

Cazetti's boots were wet and he slipped on the stone floors inside. It was ten after two in the morning. An Embassy guard, a dog-and-pony

Marine in a Delta blues uniform, spoke to Cazetti from a speaker inside a booth closed in glass.

"Hey, Marine. Can I help you?"

"I'd take a cup of coffee." Cazetti lit a cigarette.

"I meant: Marine, what are you doing there?"

"It's like this: I work for the United States government. I'm in the Armed Forces. I have important business in regard to national security."

The Embassy guard pointed to the corporal stripes on his sleeve. "You see this? I don't care."

Lieutenant Cercio came in the door.

"Ready, Cazetti. Let's go."

"Don't you want a cup of coffee, sir?"

"No. Let's go home."

They got into the jeep and started off down the corniche, an avenue with a median that followed the shoreline. It was illuminated with yellow over-lights which made the fog a mustard color. The wind was whipping at the shore in gusts, and waves were breaking on the seawall and spewing over the wall onto the road.

"I'm going to get soaked," the lieutenant said.

"Yes, sir. You are. Did you get a full slide-trombone from Joe Sfir's girl?"

"What do you know about Joe Sfir's girl?"

"I forgot I never heard of her. What's her name, sir?"

"Sondrine. How do you like that?"

"Is she pretty?"

"Oh . . . *nice.*" The lieutenant looked out the windshield with his nose close to it. He lifted and reset his soft-cover, and wiped his face. "You might meet her tomorrow in Junieh. We're going up to talk to Joe Sfir. She did this belly dance, Cazetti. Out of this world; kind of weird, but enticing. She has daring. She has *pujah.* I was strangely touched. Yes. . . . You know what I sense about this place?"

"What's that, sir?"

"Opportunity. Do you sense that?"

Cazetti thought. "Yeah."

"Just have some imagination about it. It's exotic. It's goddamned erotic. I sense we could be pioneers."

"If the war quits, sir."

"Where's the war?"

"Who knows, sir?"

"The -2 do."

"The -2 do."

The jeep rose a hill that looked over the camps, and coming down the hill at Sabra, where the black flag was still flapping, a deep pool of water had formed, so Cazetti set the four-wheel drive and opened the snorkel and they went through it. On a berm over the grave, an Italian machine-gun crew waved. The hands popped from either side of the gun like ears at either side of a face. They wore the red fez caps of the Bersaglieri. Cazetti waved back, and it seemed to Cazetti then, that whenever you toured through the ville on wheels, you could always find somebody friendly.

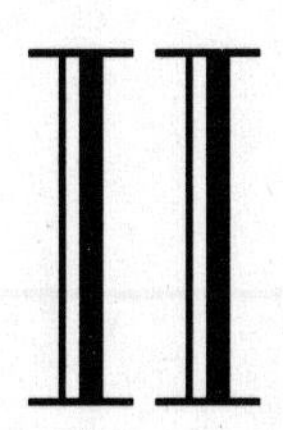

Knocked-up Mamas

THE HIGHWAY LEADING north along the coast passed through a tunnel rimmed in square stones before it came out in Junieh, a town that still belonged to the world. The storming night gave over to a fresh span of sky over the sea, and the wind blew with cheerful floating gulls. The sun was warm. The ships were farther out from shore than usual, and they looked harmless far away.

They had come up from Ashrafiey, where the streets had been crowded, where they had been given heads of lettuce and dates as presents from exited vendors, and mobs of children had screamed "Hello American!" and had tried to climb aboard the jeep when they were already five inside it. In Junieh they could park the jeep, and walk along smoking cigars with their war-belts unbuckled in front and dangling from the deuce-harnesses, and that's what they did.

They came upon a certain villa on the street which was stuccoed a cream color and had an outdoor staircase leading up to a terrace on the street. Cazetti saw the head of a small young girl with a ponytail gliding smoothly along the wall of the terrace. He could only see her head. It disappeared and appeared again gliding. The girl was singing in French. Cazetti looked up the staircase, and he could see she had on roller skates which solved the riddle of her gliding. The girl noticed him peeking, and hid behind the corner of the house. She let one eye work around the corner and she scrutinized Cazetti, then decided she was not afraid and continued to go gliding on her roller skates, singing her French song.

When it was time they rolled in to the Automobile Touring Club of Lebanon to meet Joe Sfir. There were bungalows and slow bumps, and then a set of tennis courts. Minovich called out to a man in tennis whites who was crouching, tying his sneakers and perspiring. On the other side of the net waited a woman in a pleated tennis skirt and turquoise shirt with her racket standing on her toe. She shaded her eyes to look at the jeep. She had a wide jaw and thin lips and a small chin. The man clawed the squares of the fence when he stood up to speak. He had semi-Oriental eyes, scorch-black. His brow protruded weirdly, as though there were a finger under the skin and there was an odd deep dimple at the bridge of the nose. His hair was black and curly and long enough to shake when he made a sudden movement with his head. He and Minovich traded greetings. Joe Sfir proposed a rendezvous at the pool side. Then he turned away.

"What a shiftless wanker," Lieutenant Cercio said.

"I don't know, sir," Cain replied.

Cazetti pulled forward to a guard house. The guard didn't want to let the jeep pass. Cazetti explained to him in French that they were guests of Joe Sfir, and then the guard wanted very much to let the jeep pass, and he got out of the guard house to be sure the jeep had no difficulty passing. They got out of the jeep at a group of palm trees near some steps that led down to the beach. A white fence of staves screened the pool in the garden of the clubhouse.

"Joe might not tell us all he knows," Minovich said. "But what he does tell is so far reliable."

"Women say he wanks," said Cercio.

"Secure the weapons, bud," Davey said.

"I don't go in?" asked Cazetti.

"You don't go in," Davey said.

"Cain's going in."

"Whoop-di-do," said Cain.

"Wait by the jeep and keep the weapons," Lieutenant Cercio said. "We'll send you a drink."

The weapons made a pile on the back seat in the jeep. Cazetti paced around the jeep after the others went in to the pool through an arch in the fence. Joe Sfir and his tennis partner strolled through momentarily, with a cordial attitude, their hands folded in the smalls of their backs. Music sailed from the pool. There was the sound of a single dive-splash. Sometimes the breeze carried a child's peals in the etherizing beach muffle.

A woman came along in a terry-cloth robe with wide vertical green stripes. Her black hair was pinned up under a straw hat. She had a glamorous face with pouting lips, vaguely camel-like, and fine Lebanese honeyed-cinnamon skin. Her eyes bore makeup only at the outside corners, after a French style, and she had small, darling ears in which she wore tiny diamond earrings set in silver pinwheels. Her gaze fell on Cazetti, and she came up close to the jeep.

"You're a driver?" she asked.

"That's how it is," Cazetti said. "I think you're looking for my lieutenant. Cercio. He's at the pool. You speak French?"

"Of course."

"Let's speak French." Cazetti switched to it. "How's your apartment?" He put one hand on the hood of the jeep and leaned on it.

"My apartment is very well, thank you."

"Good."

She was amused. "How is your vehicle?"

"Like this, like that. It could be happier. Your name is Sondrine?"

"Yes. That's it."

"I'd be happier if we could call you Sardine. It's cuter."

"Oh, really? Well . . ." She ran her hands down her figure and looked up, "Sardine. Perhaps. Yes, I think. It's true. It's cuter, given how I am. I like it. And for a family name, what do you think?"

Cazetti thought. He shifted on his legs and crossed them. "Dupont. It goes well in English too. Listen: Sardine Dupont."

She winced. "I prefer it in French. But I accept it. You can be happier now."

"I am happier. You want a cigarette?"

"I must go to join my lieutenant, you know. And there is, I think, a very adorable sergeant too. He's very big. He reminds me of one of your civil war generals somehow."

"You mean to say General Grant. That would be Sergeant Cain. It's true they resemble each other, a lot, except Cain doesn't have a beard, of course. I hadn't thought of that."

"I find him adorable. So big!"

"He's one of my friends," Cazetti said.

"I have a friend. Camille. Do you know her?"

"No. Not yet. Are you happy with my lieutenant?"

"Very happy. He's very dear. He's gallant."

"Oh, really?"

"Yes. You can be my friend, however. I like to have friends. I make friends very easily. You believe me. I'm sure. Because you have something that pleases me."

"Firearms, you mean?"

"No." She smiled.

Davey came back through the arch in the fence with a white towel horseshoed around his neck and a tumbler in his hand. He shook his head as he approached.

"Bud, you were told to secure from that conduct."

"Around the line companies, yeah," Cazetti said.

"Good-bye," Sardine said. She walked gracefully to the pool. Davey put his boot on the tow-bar of the jeep, and gave Cazetti the drink. Cazetti gulped from it and shivered.

"Thanks for that, Davey. Did you get a good look at that?"

"Listen, bud. Don't horn in on your looey. And she belongs to Joe Sfir anyway, so don't worry about anything else."

"How's she belong to Joe Sfir?"

"One of the things that Joe Sfir owns is a radio station. She's a disc jockey with her own show, and a big-time thing in Junieh, and she owes Joe Sfir. What she's got, is what he gives her. They go way back, and you just got here, enlisted man."

"I think you love her."

"Forget it."

"You do. You think I'm a dope?"

"I don't have that kind of cash. I don't have shiny bars on my collar."

"So what. You love her."

"You were issued a brain, right? Give your military brain a tone burst. These are Lebs, bud. Hamsters. Do you remember where you are? You're a few miles north of forty thousand corpses and ten years of civil war."

"I don't care. Her name is Sardine Dupont, a fabulous celebrity, and Staff-Sergeant Davey has a crush on her. I decided."

"Think what you want to."

"What's Joe Sfir say?" Cazetti sat down on the hood of the jeep.

"He says we've had some rain. There's going to be some fighting for winter positions, but no big action till the spring. The muftied guys are black-hat coming back from Tunis. They're getting leaked in-country with help from Syria. We'd like to know how many and where. You get it?"

"Sure."

"Cercio and Joe Sfir have got an idea about a photo-recon job for you. Maybe in Alayah. They want to screw it down with Hitman."

"Please don't say it's like another Damascus highway job, sitting in the rocks all day, waiting for Israelis. Remember that? That sucked."

"You're a Marine, bud. You can handle it."

"Yeah. But you're Counter-Intelligence, and you can make it so it doesn't suck."

Davey walked away with his head dropped, staring at the ground, bending the forelock of his hair between two fingers.

Shadows from the palms waved over the hood of the jeep and Cazetti had his back on the windshield and his legs out along the hood. He was dozing. A white Mercedes with a chauffeur parked next to the jeep, and Cazetti swiveled off the hood.

Hitman got out of the car with a soft leather briefcase in his hand.

"A feller could follow me in there, Corporal."

"I'm supposed to watch the weapons, sir."

"Put them in the back of my car."

Cazetti did that, and followed the Hitman to the pool walking at a pace behind.

Paper barrel lanterns rocked from hooks on posts around the garden and the pool. Women wrapped in silk sarongs with towels falling from the backs of their heads stepped around lounging chairs with walrus-bloated men on them.

The sun was lowering. The Intell crew were wet-headed and only partly uniformed. They were sitting at pebbled glass tables, with drinks in front of them, with Joe Sfir's crew on the porch leading into the clubhouse, where a casino glittered from within. There were gaming tables and a stage. At the corner of the stage, a fat old woman was singing a folk song through a microphone, hidden from the general view. She looked bored and smoked a cigarette while she sang, and smoke came out of her mouth, pressing through the sieve of the microphone.

Sardine had unpinned her hair and she was being witty with Lieutenant Cercio, "Yes, you know, last year I went to France and had an operation. Isn't it true, Camille?"

The woman in the tennis skirt said, "Yes, it's true. We worried."

"I had a tumor in my head, and they cut out half of my brain."

"They cut out half your brain?" the lieutenant said. "They should make you a Marine Corps officer. Yes, a field-grade officer. But then, they'd have to cut out half your spine too . . ."

"What is a field-grade?" asked Camille.

Minovich noticed Hitman and Cazetti walking in, and said, "Majors' and colonels' ranks, like this man here, Hitman Hitchins."

Joe Sfir rose when Hitman walked up to him. Lieutenant Cercio winced. Hitman bowed to the ladies, and smiled at them while he was introduced, but he didn't offer his hand. Then he flicked his head toward the casino and Joe Sfir followed him in. Cazetti sat down next to Cain.

"Can a guy get a drink?" Cazetti asked, leaning into Cain.

"Ask Camille." Cain said.

Cazetti leaned the other way, "Could you call your waiter for a drink? Do you speak French?"

"I'm afraid not very well. I'm much better at English."

Camille kept her eyes on Minovich. He had his shirt off and she looked at the scars which puckered on his ribs. She said to Cazetti, "What would you like him to bring for you?"

"I was having gin before. But I don't like it. I like scotch. Scotch, soda, rocks, large." Camille made a sharp kiss sound and a waiter in a black vest came. She spoke to him in Arabic.

Cazetti saw the Hitman and Joe Sfir turn their backs to the pool, standing at the butt end of a roulette table. He whispered to Cain, "What's that about?"

Cain put his fingers under his blouse so that only Cazetti could see them. He rubbed them together. "He's keeping Joe on our side."

Sardine dipped her finger in a flowered bowl of hummus and sucked it off her finger, looking meaningfully at Cain.

She looked at the lieutenant. "What books have you read?"

Cazetti had a curious feeling, but he couldn't pin it down. The sun was warm on his back. Davey was looking on, smiling, never blinking, and he stayed quiet. The waiter put down drinks.

"My favorite one is *War and Peace*," Lieutenant Cercio said. "I read it twice. I'm going to read it again. God, I love that book."

"Why? I wonder," Sardine said. She pinched the frond of a radish and held the radish at the tip of her lips.

"Well, I'm in the business." The lieutenant looked at her.

"We are all in that business, I think. It bores me, that business. I wish I could think of another, but they removed that part of my brain." She bit her radish.

"You know what book I read on ship?" Cazetti said, after draining half his drink and Zippoing a cigarette. "This little sniper, his name is Ballory, he gave me a picture book called *Knocked-up Mamas*." Camille flinched away from him.

"Cazetti," Davey said. He shook his head.

"What is *Knocked-up Mamas*?" Sardine asked.

"It's the weirdest thing I ever saw."

"Cazetti. Secure," Lieutenant Cercio said.

"But I want to know what it is," Sardine said.

Camille held out her hand, and Minovich took it and led her to the pool.

"Oh, sir. It won't offend her."

"I give you my permission, if it does," Sardine said. "I am decided to know what it is. Tell me it in French."

Cazetti spoke as fast as he could, "It was a book full of photographs of young girls who were pregnant and they had nothing on except black boots up to here and they were doing house chores like cooking and watering the lawn." He grabbed Cain's arm with both hands.

Sardine burst out in squeals. Her hair fell over her forehead. She pulled it back with her ring finger and her thumb, but left some of it sticking to the corner of her mouth.

"La pelouse!" Her face was flushed. "It is insane and vulgar. Terribly vulgar. I absolutely adore it. Oh, Lieutenant." She grabbed Lieutenant Cercio by the leg. "I must have a copy of this book. I'm going to talk about it on the radio."

"I don't understand," the lieutenant said. "You want a copy of *Knocked-up Mamas*?"

Hitman and Joe Sfir came back to the table, and Joe Sfir sat down. Hitman stayed standing there with the briefcase under his arm.

"What is so funny here?" he asked.

"I can't believe it, sir," the lieutenant said. He held Sardine by the shoulder. "She wants me to get her a copy of a book called *Knocked-up Mamas*."

"So?" Hitman asked.

"Well, sir. It's something pretty raunchy."

"Lieutenant." He took the briefcase from his side and slapped his leg with it, "Don't make fun of *Knocked-up Mamas*."

"No, sir,"

"Some of my best friends . . ."

"Read *Knocked-up Mamas*, sir?"

"No lieutenant. They knock mamas up."

Hitman bowed and walked away to the beach, dragging Joe Sfir with him by a simple slant of his head.

Minovich sat with Camille on one of the lounging chairs at the edge of the porch. They shared it. They looked back at the laughter going on at the tables. Camille made a worried remark about Cazetti, which he heard. But Minovich reassured her by saying it was just Cazetti, who was just sort of like that, but nothing she should worry about while the officers were around.

"I have a certain feeling," said Camille, "that something is wrong with this. I sensed something."

"What do you think it is?" asked Minovich. "It's not me, I hope."

"I'm sure it's not you. You give me a good feeling. I'd like to confess that to you."

"That I'm glad of," said Minovich. He started to button up his blouse. Camille took the buttons herself and worked on them slowly.

"You're a heroic man, I'd say. That's my sense of you. It shows. I mean, that you've survived a lot. It attracts me to you."

"You mean the scars on my gut. Those are old."

"Still, they're yours. Do you know what Lebanese girls are like?"

"What do you mean? In bed?"

"No. What should make us different there? I mean our character. We have rather a pronounced affection for strength, for what survives. We like to pick out heroes for ourselves."

"No way. Not so. I got shot in Vietnam in 1968. I'd like to never get shot again. I'm hanging on to what I've got, with what I've got. That's all."

Camille finished with his buttons. "Don't you see what I mean? I mean the war is awfully hard, and it goes on and on. I worry I would die in it. A feeling came through me. It was a fateful feeling. It was very melancholy."

Minovich looked back at the tables, then set his face again squared up to Camille. He got his hand on top of her crossed knee. "I know that feeling," Minovich said. He kissed her.

The old woman had finished singing her folk songs. She sat down with a glass of *arack* and stared, turning an ashtray around and around. Nobody bothered to talk to her. The sun was dropping behind the curve of the sea. There was a square of wood parquet in the middle of the gaming tables which the waiter switched red spotlights on. There was music with the sound of jazz clarinets.

"I think your driver is mischievous," Sardine said.

"That's kind of you to say," the lieutenant said.

"He don't know when to secure," Davey said.

"No. He is sweet. However, I would not want to let him take me for a dance. He probably would ravish me. Lieutenant?"

"Of course. Let's go."

They went dancing. Cazetti and Cain looked at each other, and they looked at Davey. Davey walked over to the bartender and gave him money. He came back with a bottle.

"Come with me, enlisted ones," he said.

Cain and Cazetti followed him out to the jeep where they got dressed up again in weapons. They sat on the hood and drank from the bottle. The hitman took a sip of it when he appeared and then disappeared in his car. It was night and the officers were still inside. When they were drunk, they sang:

She had long black hair
And ruby red lips
And great big tits.
She was a primadonna
From Beirut, Lebanon.

The enlisted ranks of the colonel's headquarters staff lived in the cellar of a mangled rectangular concrete building, previously occupied by the Syrian 85th commando regiment. Israeli air strikes had blasted it to a honeycomb form of upright rubble. It stretched in a line parallel to the beach between the Battalion Headquarters, a hundred yards to the south, and the supply unit and artillery battery a hundred yards to the north. Its entry faced the back of the COC, separated by a quadrangle in which stood a line of burned-out buses and loops of concertina wire.

Cazetti staggered down a blown hallway lit by a dangling bulb. The light swayed on walls with red and black swirls of Arabic graffiti. Machine-gun fire was distant. He dropped down the stairway leading to the cellar and crashed into a support column that had bloodstains on it. It was semi-dark in the cellar, wheezing with the sounds of the half-sleeping troops. There was a crowd of cots with peaked tents of mosquito net. Ponchos hung on comm-wires. The floor was littered with flak jackets, steelpots, bandoleers and magazines, rifles, Alice packs, boots, cases of C-rats. A candle glowed off the floor where Mangas was dressing for guard duty and Cicchelero was eating from a can with his elbows on his knees.

Mangas pulled Cazetti down to sit on his cot. "We got the Rover Patrol in twenty minutes. You and me do."

"My lieutenant has a mistress," Cazetti said.

"You're drunk." Mangas stretched a watch cap over the stiff half-inch bristles of his black hair.

"That's correct. But this is wonderful. Listen to how wonderful."

"You know about Yuck and all that," Mangas said. "They put you on charges, my friend."

"Who cares? Listen to about my lieutenant's mistress: Her name is Sondrine, but her real name is Sardine Dupont. She has an apartment near the University, on the hill over the Embassy. We made up a song. And it's beautiful. You can hear her, on the Phalange radio station. And Gunner Minovich has a girl up in Junieh. Another thing, he decided to go to the Embassy for the paperwork to pull her out. It's all so fine."

"How much liquor did you doggone have, my friend?"

"Shut up or I'll punch you. Listen to how wonderful. The Counter-Intell guys put Joe Sfir on the payroll. Hitman did, and Minovich. And these girls are his pals, they're his entourage because Joe Sfir owns the radio station and everything else in Junieh. He's a wonderful man."

"You know what you're doggone saying? You're saying *our* Intell guys are sleeping with Leb spies and the guy who set it all up is getting paid for it. That's how it is. That's pure and simple. Don't be stupid."

"No, no, no. You're stupid. You suspect the worst in people. You're analytical. I hate when you analyze something. If you do that again, I'll punch you."

"Come on, Cazetti. These people are totally desperate. Their country is chopped and shot to pieces. Who is using who? You see?"

A red glow appeared in the corner when Cicchelero dragged on a cigarette. The sound of a furtive unwrapping of foil began from the corner.

"We're using them," Cazetti said. "We're the ones. Because why? Because there's a war on. I saw it. That's a wonderful thing. And there's a fabulous woman in it. Or do you want a punch?"

"I don't want a punch. Cicchelero does. That guy is eating again."

"Yo. Don't be saying that."

"What are you eating?"

"Shit-disk," Cicchelero said.

"Where'd you get that shit-disk?" Mangas said. "You moused in the chow again."

"I saved a B-3."

"You saved a B-3? You didn't draw a B-3. So how did you save it? Tell me how many meals you think you rate in one day."

"I rate a B-3. A B-3 I rate."

Mangas walked over to the glow in the corner and reached into Cicchelero's pack. He drew out a handful of chocolate wheels wrapped in tin foil. "Where'd you get all these?"

"I saved them. I save all my B-3's."

"My friend, I'm taking these. After all the beers I bought you, this is what you do?"

"Yo. Then I paid you back, if you take them."

Mangas sighed. "Never trust a man who pays back in shit-disks."

"Hey," Cazetti said. "I'm on charges?"

Mangas and Cazetti began to patrol in the compound, carrying the rifles by the handles, holding canteen cups of coffee. They moved in the dark, and poked the black corners of the buildings and the bunkers. Cazetti tried teaching the new song to Mangas and that annoyed

Mangas. They wandered around the generators and the wires. A set of headlights came down the airport road and turned into the perimeter, and stopped at the guard post there. A surge of shouting burst at the scene where the figures of men, caught in the headlights, appeared to be flailing arms. Mangas and Cazetti began to run.

"Lock and load?"

"I don't know? Let's just go," Mangas said.

The white Mercedes from the ATC was idling with the driver inside it. Hitman was standing with his arms cocked yelling at two black battery grunts at the guard post.

"Shot! You don't know what shot *is*! Shoot *me?* Say it again, grunt!"

"No sir," said the grunt.

Hitman's voice tore out on the other, "Did you hear me say 'Say it again?'"

"Yes, sir."

"I said, '*Did* you!'"

"No, sir." The grunt gave his partner a fearful look.

Hitman pointed at the other guard. "What did this one say?"

Mangas and Cazetti stood behind the Hitman's car. They released the magazines from the rifles carefully.

The grunt started to shake and stammer. "He said, sir, that you could get shot that way."

Hitman turned to the other, and drew his pistol, "Then say it again, grunt! Say it to *me*! Now!"

"No, sir."

"I could get shot?" Hitman hollered. "Did you say that to me?"

"Yes, sir," the grunt said.

Hitman dropped the pistol into his face. "What unit are you with?"

"Charlie Battery, sir." The grunt trembled.

"You *look* like artillery-clam! Do you know what shot is?"

"No, sir!"

Hitman grabbed the collar of the grunt's blouse. "Do you want to find out?"

"No, sir!"

"I said, do you want to?"

"No, sir!"

Hitman shook him. "Shoot who? Shoot who?"

"Nobody! Nobody, sir!"

"Very goddamn well," Hitman said. He let go the blouse collar of the trembling grunt and shouldered his pistol. He shooed his car away with a throw of his hand. He turned and walked off to the COC in the dark.

Cazetti and Mangas walked up to the guards.

Mangas tore off his watch cap and rubbed his head with the flat of his hand. The guards paced in tight circles, running their thumbs up and down the slings of their rifles, saying "Oh, man . . . Oh, man . . . Oh, man . . ."

"That is Hitman Hitchins," Cazetti said to the guards. "He's got something lurking in his heart. He's wonderful."

Christmas was observed ashore. Everybody hated it. Everybody wished it was ignored. Nobody minded going on duty or going on patrol or pulling watch or guard duty somewhere. Nobody minded any more than they always did. And once they pulled their duty, they were glad to go about their military business, especially on Christmas, when whoever was on duty had the feeling of being vigilant and useful, and in-it with the others who were vigilant and useful. It was a way to avoid the pathetic gestures of the holiday, lining up at length around the mess tents, 'One steak, One beer, Merry Christmas, Happy New Year, Move Along, Marine'. . . It was a way to avoid the embarrassment of the corny visits then from the USO and Washington men, who weren't in-it. They came, and they created, without meaning to, a divide between the in-country and the clueless. They didn't mean to be clueless and sickening. They couldn't help it. They had no clues, they weren't in-it, and it was Christmas. Also, the weather was dreary. Time sucked into the weak winter sun.

"Valuable," Cazetti said. "This is Hitman."

The radio hissed and a tone burst came back, "Roger, Hitman this is Valuable. Go ahead."

"Be advised: Hitman is okay at poz."

They were at the Lebs-2 in Ba'abda near a traffic circle. A Lebanese panhard was parked between the circle and the Lebs-2. A soldier with his torso sticking out of the cupola was reading a newspaper in the sunshine. Traffic swirled around. Machine-gun fire came from below the roundabout, from Sidon road. Israeli tanks were reconnoitering the Hooterville by firing into buildings in order to provoke the inhabitants into firing back. Cazetti and the Hitman had come through the fire and a grenade had been thrown at the jeep. Hitman walked into the Lebs-2 to find out who threw it.

A grinning Lebanese soldier with a backslung AK-47 hailed Cazetti from the top of the stairs in front of the building. Cazetti walked to the stairs and folded his arms. *"Marhaba."*

The soldier towered over him. "I speak English. I learned in school. They teach Arabic in the American school?"

"No."

"America is happy and crazy, yes? You see Israeli on the Sidon road?"

"Israeli and Phalange," Cazetti said.

"You were in Vietnam?"

"No."

"Maybe soon." The soldier sat on the stairs. "Sit down."

Cazetti sat with him. They looked out and they could see the ships in the water.

"I am a bodyguard," the soldier said. "You are a bodyguard?"

"That's right. For Hitman."

"You have strong arms."

"I know."

"Hitman is a very good man. You are proud to be his bodyguard, yes? You will get shot, yes? I was shot four times. And you?"

"Once."

"It was in Beirut?"

"No. It was in Pomona. That's in New York. You know New York?"

"Everyone knows New York. But you can get

shot in Beirut. Maybe soon. We know the mathematic. You can have Khalashnikov."

The soldier rubbed his rifle butt. Hitman and a Lebs-2 officer stood in the doorway. They were speaking in Arabic. They laughed and shook hands. Hitman and Cazetti boarded the jeep.

"Where to, sir?"

"A feller could head downtown. I've got to see some things."

They rolled out and headed toward the Green Line and the Museum Crossing.

"Sir, what's the situation? What's the mathematic?"

"Everybody's at loggerheads, and at odds, and there are points of contention. All right?"

"Because it's holy war, right, sir?"

"Who told you that?" Hitman said.

"I read it. In a newspaper. Who tried to hit us, sir?"

"Lebs-2 thinks it was the Palestinian backdrift. But it could be Amal, Druze, Mourabitoune."

"If we get hit, sir, we pull a hasty withdrawal under fire, get a combat action ribbon, and go home and get laid. Right?"

"No. Who told you that? Did you graduate from Parris Island?"

"Yes, sir."

"We get hit, we hit back, we hang on and keep on hitting, unless you want to die. The mathematic here is that one in five is going to die on us, Cazetti."

"Is that for sure, sir?"

"In this town, a feller would see much death."

They pulled up to a mansion with high black wrought-iron fencing across from the Museum Crossing and the Hippodrome where the French were camped.

"What's this place, sir?"

"It's the Ice House, Cazetti, where they keep fresh intelligence on ice." Hitman swigged from a pewter hip flask and walked past the guards into the building.

A line of tied and blindfolded prisoners was led by a rope into the back of a waiting truck. The fronts of the shirts of the prisoners were bloody. Cazetti looked on at that. A guard noticed him looking on at it. The guard smiled at Cazetti and drew his finger across his throat.

Across the street were the gates of the French camp with sandbagged turrets for guards on either side. A multiwheeled armored vehicle was rolling out from the camp. The flat carriage behind the cab was filled with journalists, strapped with cameras and sound recording gear. Their faces showed enthusiasm. Their heads snapped about with a thrill of place. This particular tingle of the circumstances betrayed each passenger, except for one. Sardine.

Cazetti waved, but she didn't notice him. He sat in the jeep.

After a span, Hitman returned, swigging from his hip flask. He offered it to Cazetti.

"Thanks, sir."

"A feller couldn't see a creepier place than that."

"Sir," Cazetti said, "I just saw Sardine. You know who I mean, sir?"

"You too?"

"I don't get you, sir."

"In the Ice House, she paid a visit. That's what my contact just told me there. Joe Sfir's girl?"

"Yes, sir. She was on a French sled with a bunch of journalists."

"That interests me. Let's go."

Cazetti hit the starter. "Sir, where to?"

"Let's go around the camps."

When the jeep was moving, Hitman said, "By the way, Davey told me about the song you all piped up at the ATC."

"He did, sir? Did he sing it?"

"He just said the words. And he said you used to be a Chevtone."

"A few years ago. That's right, sir. But I cannot believe you ever heard of the Chevtones, sir. Unless you're from New York, there's no way."

"No. I never did. Davey told me. Did you ever do 'Wonderful Dream'?"

"No, sir. The parts are too high for the Chevtones. It's a girls' song. I like it too, but the Chevtones were a bassy group."

"A feller could do it bassy. It would be good, bassy."

Cazetti shrugged. "We didn't do it, sir."

The jeep came into the woody area near Shatila camp on the central road. Cazetti moved the jeep along slowly so that Hitman could study the place. He was looking at piles of old tires and junk heaps in view.

"They make sign language out of the junk pile and stack the tires in a certain way."

"Can you read the sign language, sir?"

"No. Can you read tea leaves?"

"No, sir."

They got back to headquarters when the air was a dark swaddling gray color with looming rain in the twilight. They pulled up to the COC.

"Tell Comm you need a radio."

Hitman walked into the COC and spoke to Davey and Garces in the doorway. Rotor-chop from helicopters flying low slapped over the compound, the machine guns were slack in the doors. When they passed and it was calm again, the jeep engine ticking as it cooled could be heard in the jeep park. Neale and Mangas were batting a tennis ball with their rifle butts. Cazetti watched the other drivers, perched on the hoods of their jeeps. Davey and Garces came forward.

"We got something for you, bud, and it don't suck," Davey said.

"Pack your trash, promptly, and come back to the COC," Garces said.

"Okay," Cazetti replied.

Davey turned to Neale and said, "Go to Comm and get me a radio."

Neale hopped down from his jeep. "In the plain, or you want it secure? And do you care how old it is?"

"Secure," Davey said. "Do what you can for new."

Cazetti and Neale went about it.

Cazetti came into the COC with his pack and field gear, bandoleer, rifle, an old PRC-77 radio in his free hand. Behind the Intell partition, the colonel was standing with Hitman and Lieutenant Cercio. Minovich and Cain, with the rest of the crew, drew back and sat on mount-out boxes. Cazetti unlocked an aluminum case which held the long-range recon camera and he assembled it while standing next to Cain, who held his rifle for him. The colonel's hands traced over a tac-map with acetate overlays. Canteen cups of coffee steamed off the field desks.

"Northbound traffic on that road, I don't care about it," the colonel said. "That's all headed to the Bekaa Valley, and none of that belongs to me. Those are Israeli grids with Syrian 85th in front of them."

Hitman said, "Now, the Ice House says there is southbound movement, Colonel. There's gooners coming down this gorge by night. Joe Sfir says the Phalange in Ba'abda have confiscated mortar tubes as close as Wadi-Shur.

"Just so," said Minovich. He spat into a beer can.

Hitman continued, "This whole ridge is Druze, with one or two pockets of Maronite life. Israeli poz, here; at Bhamdoun, keeps all that Syrian mechanized hardware up in the Bekaa. Israelis also have positions at Al-quamatiya, here. And Arayyat."

"My focus is here, gentlemen," the colonel said. "In Alayah. We can handle the drip-down with the line companies, but when the Israelis pull back to the Awali River, a vacuum forms." The colonel used a red marker to draw on the overlays. "As we are, here, these two roads threaten me. The question is what kind of gooners take up the Israeli positions and control these two roads. I will not have my ass in a sling, gentlemen. I will not have a Syrian mechanized division pounding me from this ridge."

"Sir, we want to recon from Alayah."

"You bet you do, Lieutenant," the colonel said.

"What we could do, sir, is stick Cazetti up there to recon the movement."

"I want that a safe observation post. You make it a good one. I will not get caught up in trading for hostages. Is that understood?"

"Yes, sir," Lieutenant Cercio said.

Minovich spat again and stood up to speak. "We parlayed a safe poz through Joe Sfir and his connections with the Maronites. There's a hilltop monastery . . . here." He pointed to a speck in Alayah on the map. "Nobody's interfered with them, so far, and the field of view is excellent."

"Maronite monks go armed sometimes, I understand," the colonel said. "They do in Tyre."

Minovich shot a glance at Hitman, who refolded his arms. "These are noncombatants, sir," Hitman said.

The colonel thought, pulling on the wattles of his throat, "Okay. Very well. Run him up there when it's dark." He turned around to Cazetti. "Stand up." He grabbed Cazetti by the green bandage cloth around his neck. "You call in. And you come home. You don't get your ass in the sling. If you bother me with an incident I have to administrate, you're going to the brig, for past charges and any new ones I can think of. You understand?"

"Yes, sir," said Cazetti.

"And you, gentlemen," the colonel said, "do not lose my duty-flick."

It was dark then. Headlights traced around the runways. Joe Sfir's white Mercedes idled on the airport road against a fence of iron spears. Some automatic fire spattered in the Hooterville but it could not be seen. Hitman and Minovich put magazines in their AK-47s opening the doors, and Davey helped Cazetti get into the back seat of the car with his gear.

"Bud," Davey said. "One thing: There's no monks where you're going to, so keep your conduct secure. Say the word."

"Secure," Cazetti said.

"The colonel's serious about the brig."

"I know. Secure. Secure."

They drove out into the city and the rain came down. The car filled up with blue smoke from cigarettes and the windows fogged from body heat. The driver wiped the windshield with his sleeve pinched in his paw and the car went up into the hills. Sometimes Hitman spoke to him in Arabic.

They came along the ridgeline road in Alayah and drizzle was caught in the branches of the towering cedars there and hit the windshield in splats of water shaken loose from the boughs. The road was cratered from artillery and the headlights caught the ripping splinter marks the shrapnel made around the craters and against a crumbled stone wall to the side.

The wall made an angle away from the road and led to a set of iron doors, hinged directly to the stones of the wall. The doors, which were solid and heavy, closed together in the center. The car stopped.

On the left, a rope poked through the sheet of metal. The driver got out and yanked on it. A bell clanged from within.

"Radio in," Hitman said.

Cazetti radioed. "Valuable, be advised: Big-eye is okay at poz."

They stood outside the car waiting for the

doors to open. The flare of a flashlight peeked under the door. There was heard a foot plunk into a puddle and the sound of a little gasp, eminently feminine.

Minovich said, "Do a good job. And be secure, Cazetti. They all speak French."

The door opened and there stood, in the dark, the two nuns Cazetti recognized from the hospital party.

"Please stay seated," Joe Sfir said.

The old nun said the same thing to him, but they were not sitting and they did not sit down.

The driver opened the trunk of the car and brought out boxes of medical supplies marked with red crosses and labels in French. Minovich and Hitman helped the driver carry them inside the doors. The young nun, Philomena, fetched a dented wheelbarrow streaked with crusted white residues. The medical supplies were stacked in it.

"I do not think the arms may enter the enclosure," the old nun said. "That offers us a certain risk." She kept the flashlight pointed at her sandaled feet.

"She's got a problem with the rifle, sir," Cazetti whispered to the Hitman.

"Tell her you will not be disarmed, but tell her gently," Hitman said.

"You see," Cazetti said, picking his way through logically, "we have a tradition; it's that we sleep with our rifles. It is only a symbolic thing. But traditions can't be broken. Or else God gets angry. Isn't that so? I would never, never shoot off this rifle. No. It's only in case there's a journalist. I'm here to look at the country. And to be your guest and your friend. But to break a tradition is bad luck. Where could this rifle sleep, if not with me?"

The old nun heaved a sigh and touched her wrist to her forehead. "You tire me. All right, close the gates."

"I told you. They speak French," Minovich said. "Keep your radio on. Give us an hour and call us."

The officers and Joe Sfir turned out the doors and Philomena closed them. She lifted the handles of the wheelbarrow and rolled it off quickly toward a light hanging under a portico where there was a padlocked door.

"Follow me, please," the old nun said. She walked across the courtyard with the flashlight low. Cazetti followed. The ground smelled of moist chicken straw. He perceived an enormous crag of a building ahead. The glow of the city lights faintly skylined it, and at one end a bell tower rose. A heroic crucifix in the center of the yard stood over his head on the round base of a pedestal with stones strewn around it.

"You sleep up there."

"In the tower?" Cazetti asked.

"Yes," said the old nun.

After the radio contact, Cazetti spread out his gear in the tower. The tower was open on all sides with arches supporting the cupola. Through the center a rocking beam supported the bells. There was a large bell with the name "Maria" engraved, surmounted by three little crosses, and a small bell named "Therese." There was an ample square of floor from which the bells could be touched. Cazetti touched the bells. Stairs plunged down a shaft.

His sleeping bag was stained and oily. It smelled, in a way, like meat. Cazetti took off his boots and sat with his legs in the bag, his back against one of the arches. One of the plates in his flak jacket pinched at his back, so he took it off and stood it around the radio as if the radio were wearing it. He opened a can of fruit cocktail and drank the juice, then tumbled the fruit into his mouth, tapping the butt of the can.

"This is skate," he thought. He lay down inside his cozy bag, looking up at the inside of the cupola and the stars through the arches. He was happy to be where he was. He was amazed to be near the nun who had touched him with her singing. He thought, she might get into some kind of situation and sing again. He thought, nobody had ever kissed her. She was charming. This was not secure, he thought. He made himself dismiss the idea. He thought for a while about Sardine, how she looked exciting and devilish, especially while laughing. He conjured her in devilish ways, and soon he fell asleep.

A kind of groaning woke him up in the dark. He slurped at drool from the corner of his mouth and flinched, sitting up. He looked around without moving his head. His right arm prickled him fiercely. He listened. There didn't seem to be a sound. Then there was a sound again. It was like a groaning, but it was a tone. It was a pretty tone. Then it was clear the nuns were singing. He unstrapped the cover of his watch. It was 3:30.

He had never looked down upon a firefight. He had always seen them from a low angle. There was a small one under way in Shuwayfat. He could see the tracers fly in a peculiar little pool of action. He took the binoculars and set his arms against the low parapet. The view danced in the glass. Silent flames fluttered out of the windows of a couple of the buildings. The perimeter around the runways was still. The Navy ships were visible, and mute. They were shadows, merely, hovering off the shore.

Cazetti could hear portions of the singing while he lay on his belly looking down at the firefight and the places he knew in the city. He felt secure, and he slept again.

Morning light came through the boughs of the cedars of the ridge. Cazetti screened it with the haze of his eyelashes and stayed lying down with his head on his arm. He wanted to delay his military day. The radio quietly hissed.

"I know a proverb that is very beautiful, and it has to do with someone who enters a monastery in the rain. It's important, at least I think it is. At least, it's very beautiful. You speak French, isn't that so?"

Cazetti saw Philomena standing on the stairs with her head at the level of the floor. Her nose was cheerfully pointing around as she spoke, words tumbling headlong out of her mouth in French. Cazetti blinked and sat up. He didn't mean to, but he scowled at her.

"There are many proverbs that are true." She stepped up the stairs. She was holding a wicker tray with a plate and a pot on it. "'With your eyes upon the crucifix, you see what the world would do to God. With your eyes upon Our Lady, you see what God would do to the world.' I find that the Russian proverbs are very reliable. But I don't think they sound very beautiful in Russian. The communists shot the czar, you know, and he was a saint. All the beauty that existed in holy Russia they destroyed after that. Get up, eh?"

"Tell me your name," Cazetti said.

She scowled, feeling her patience tried. "I'm Philomena. You know that. Don't play." She stamped a foot.

Cazetti peeled himself out of the bag. Philomena slid the tray onto the floor and finished rising the steps. The floor was cold through his socks, so Cazetti stood on the toe of the bag where the letters "U.S." were stamped. He put his hands in his pockets and yawned.

The tray had two items rolled in bread. Around the rolls, small cuttings from the bough of a cedar made a garnish, and petals of a wildflower were placed along the tops of the rolls.

"These are *shuarma,*" said Philomena. "They are poor ones, I'm sorry. There's no lamb. We don't have lamb in the house, except at Easter. This is tea." She drew her finger inside the kerchief that clung about her face to be sure it was clinging in a proper way.

"I saw you once," Cazetti said. "At the hospital of the Phalange."

"Yes. I remember. I put Kalil there next to you. I said to myself, 'Who will be gentle towards Kalil?' and so I decided on you. And then he was *drunk* in the end. I was very deceived. You deceived Our Lady."

"What are you talking about? Excuse me, I deceived you?"

"Of course you did. . . . You were not loving, and you were supposed to be. Of course you knew that, but you made Kalil drunk so that you could behave however you wished."

"And who are *you*, first of all?" Cazetti was getting angry.

Philomena dropped her cowl down around her shoulders. The white asprin crown with the blue cross tilted about with her head. She tucked the stem of her crucifix in its pouch and ducked under the large bell. She came closer to Cazetti. Her big girlish brown eyes fixed him. Her hands sprung and twittered, "Evidently Our Lady wants you to be very different from what you are. It's not her fault; she's like that. She loves you. But you are deceptive because you have no love. Nothing connects your emptiness to God.

You have a soul like the gerbil hiding in a little rock cave. So I will show you how to love Our Lady very much, and she will take you to God." Philomena gestured with her hand as though to dangle an invisible treat in front of Cazetti's face. "Come out here, little gerbil. Come out! You see? That's it: I'm going to give birth to you."

"You have some *psychiatric* problems. Calm yourself!" Cazetti reached for a cigarette from his cargo pouch. He lit it and moved away from Philomena. "You don't know who you're talking to, you have psychiatric problems, you're probably an orphan with a traumatic condition."

"You see very little. That's sad," Philomena said while she moved closer to Cazetti again. "I'll explain for you. I'm very *feconde,* you see? I have children everywhere, even in Brazil. I mean spiritual children, of course. I am very *feconde*. That is a grace Our Lord confided to me. That's why I am happy. I will give birth to you."

"You are wrong," Cazetti said, "You are a nuisance. You are a Sicilian. You are a bad nun."

Philomena laughed at him. "No. Why do you say all that? I have been a nun a long time now, since I was a *toute petite.* You will see. You will be my child and I will throw you into the lap of Our Lady. Like that. I am very *feconde.*"

"Listen: You get away."

The small bell in the tower began to rock back and forth. Philomena automatically fell on her knees. She yanked on Cazetti's blouse-tails to make him kneel. He wouldn't.

"It's the Angelus," she said, and she scowled.

She began to sing the Angelus in French, and Cazetti felt that it would be easier not to resist her, and he knelt, holding the cigarette behind his back. He scratched his head more than it itched. He was relieved when the singing stopped.

Cazetti passed days in the bell tower photographing military vehicles and uniformed or muftied troops on the roads leading south and east from the ridge. He left the tower only to use a latrine near the goat pens, which he didn't like. He didn't like goats, and the latrine was not private enough, and chickens threatened him when he was vulnerable.

Pieces of 130mm artillery were being towed by Soviet trucks and they were going south. Jeeps with old 106mm recoilless rifles were coming down from the northeast. There were motley half-uniformed troops which Cazetti could not identify and muftied men with AK-47s slithering down the ravine lying south of the tower. At times Israeli tanks went north on the roads, but there was an obvious trend to the movement in the unhappiest way. He radioed it in to Garces, who plotted the activity on the tac-maps. The singing in the morning woke him. He liked it.

Philomena sometimes would sit with him when she brought up trays of tea and the gracious, decorated gestures of food. The food was bad food. It made Cazetti worry about dysentery. He threw it away in the latrine and sustained himself with C-rats. Philomena admonished him about eating out of cans. "We were made for a certain beauty," she said. She didn't like him cooking or shaving in his helmet either, for the same reason. But Cazetti looked forward to her company, and had an agony of always expecting her, of always keeping his gear looking right in case she came. When she was not there, he was grumpy, and he was growing anxious about her while he watched the encroachment and the movement, hostile and strengthening. He knew the mathematic and he knew that action would open in Alayah. He didn't feel she was secure. He began thinking up ways to get her to linger when she came up the stairs. He tried interesting her in the radio, in the camera, the binoculars. She had no interest in any of it, except his first-aid pack. Her interest was to relieve him of it as quickly as she could, and then she bolted with it.

Cazetti thought of another approach then to coax her into lingering. He faked an interest in *her* things.

"What is that thing you have on your thumb?"

"This is a *dizanier,*" she said. "I use it when I pray for you." She brightened. She leaned towards him.

"Oh really? How do you use it?"

"On the little cross, I say the Our Father. I close my eyes. The ten little beads make a circle. Those are the Hail Marys. I picture you coming out of the rock cave and sitting on the lap of Our Lady, and I say the Hail Marys. That's it."

"Why do you do that?"

"Don't be stupid."

"What else do you have?"

"I have my Rosary, of course."

"Where do you have it?"

"Here. On my belt. Are you being stupid?"

"No. Of course. I see it."

"I hope you pray for me. Will you do that?"

"What for?" Cazetti asked.

"Well . . . for my radical conversion!"

"Why do you need a radical conversion? You're a nun. You're radical."

"You see very little, it is so sad. You must, you must pray for my radical conversion."

"Okay. Calm yourself."

There was a pause, and she smiled at him. She rubbed the top of her head. The radio was hissing, then a tone burst came. Lieutenant Cercio's voice followed the burst.

"Big-eye, Big-eye, this is Redman-2, over."

Cazetti reached behind Philomena to grab the handset and lie down to speak, "Redman-2, Big-eye, over."

"Big-eye, be advised, Hitman is en route to your poz. Hitman will extract you. Eighty-six your poz in fifteen mikes. Clear?"

Philomena looked down over her left shoulder at Cazetti.

"Roger that," Cazetti said, looking at her. "Big-eye out." He sat up. "I have to go. I want to know something."

"What?" She asked.

"Can you leave here? Are you allowed to leave this place?"

"This is not a prison. Of course we are allowed to leave. We do not want to leave here."

"But you have to leave here. You are not secure."

"Of course we are secure. This is a house which belongs to Our Lady. No harm can come to us here. Our Lady would never permit it. It would not be respectful to her son."

"Listen," Cazetti said. He stood up and started gathering his gear. "The troops going down that road don't believe that."

"But who?"

"A Druze, for example. A Palestinian."

"Well, Our Lady is sorry they do not believe, but she will protect us whether or not they believe. For example, once, when I was a little girl, I was walking in the woods in France. A big black dog came growling at me . . . I made the sign of the cross and he ran away. Like that. And this dog did not believe in Our Lady and her divine son."

"I think this is different. This village will be attacked. There will be fighting here. We don't know what army will capture it."

Philomena dropped her head in her hand and thought. Momentarily she looked up, and her hands went to trembling and her nose pointing. "That is not different at all. A dog or an army is the same thing to Our Lady. She gave birth to Our Lord who is omnipotent, and she is the most intelligent woman who was ever conceived. She can always think of something."

"Don't talk like a *freak,*" Cazetti said, slipping the word "freak" out in English.

"What I said is true. What is a *frique*?"

"You! It's what you are. It's a person in the circus. You laugh when you look at a freak."

"You are welcome to laugh at me, certainly."

"Listen. Do you know what a position is in the military sense? This place is one of them. This is a strong position. Someone will want to take this place from you. If somebody wanted to fire at the Americans from here, well, maybe Our Lady would not like it, but I know my colonel would never allow it. He would destroy this place."

"What you say, they already tried that. The Druze came. They would put their little cannons here, and they said to Sister Dorothe, 'We will give you honorable martyrs and cut off your heads.' But Our Lady decided we were still too young for martyrs, and nothing happened. I assure you."

"I have to go," Cazetti said. "I don't care about the others. Tell me: Can *you* leave here?"

Philomena looked at him with her eyes narrowed and her lips tightened. "Why?"

"Why? Why I want to know if you can leave, alone, and you want to know why I want to know that . . ."

"Yes," she said. "Why?"

Cazetti shouldered the radio and the rest of his gear. His hands fidgeted. He picked up his helmet by the chinstrap.

"I want to know, I suppose, if you can be a normal woman . . . if . . . if you can be *my* woman. That's it."

He looked at her but he did not see that she understood him. Her head tilted and her eyes looked at her knees. Then she gasped. She was horrified. She bolted down the stairs.

Cazetti hit himself in the forehead with his thumb knuckle a half dozen times. He shrugged his gear more securely. He went down the tower stairs and walked into the yard on his way to the doors. The yard was bright in the sun. The stone walls were creased with shadows and the lit surfaces shimmered and Cazetti had to squint. There was a dreadful silence inside the walls. The radio faintly hissed on his shoulder. His boots made noise in the hushed yard. He wanted to be extracted from that place.

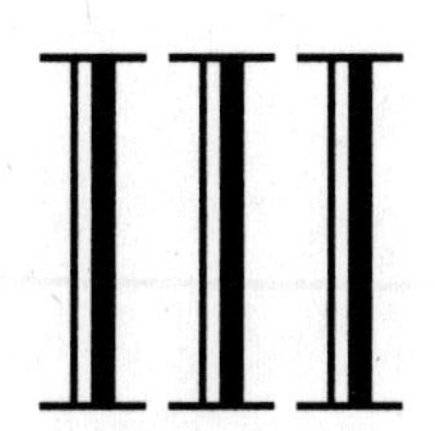

It Was Only a Story

THE MUEZZIN calls from the minaret at the blown mosque carried in the air from bullhorn speakers that gave a tinny, echoing character to the cantillations. It was eerie. Time was marked by this faithful wailing in the lulls of the days. There were signs of spring. Minovich made friends with the crew of one of the amphibious assault vehicles, which were called Tracs. They were parked outside the Battalion Headquarters, where Counter-Intelligence slept. The Tracs were not useful in the unit's disposition. Their large, windowless troop-carrying bays, which were locked by steel doors, were not used, since everyone was already ashore. They sat parked around at places with their machine guns in sleep angles. Minovich provided a case of vodka for the crew of one of these. Camille sometimes came down from Junieh. She became familiar with the amphibious assault vehicle. Minovich spoke to Lieutenant Cercio, and Camille spoke to Sardine. That was how Sardine came to be familiar with the amphibious assault vehicle. Cain was the lookout.

Yuck recovered in the Battalion Aide Station. He got in touch with his friend named Platt who worked for Yoches in the Motor-T. Platt was from Wakini, Kansas.

They conceived an ambush to take place near the latrine. It didn't go the way they wanted. Platt stubbed himself against a low-angled piss tube, not hard enough to fall, but enough to freeze up and cry "Dern!" Cazetti put him down with a punch in the throat, a knee to the groin, a fist in the face three times, and that left Yuck with his dukes up, nodding his head, looking determined. Afterwards Yuck went back again to recover in the Battalion Aide Station, with his friend Platt.

Cazetti didn't have scruples about kicking a man when he was down, or two men either. If he had not kicked them the way he had, the charges would not have stuck, but as it happened, he was busted and sent to the brig for thirty days.

Lieutenant Cercio requested permission to

take Cazetti in his custody, to then surrender him to the Military Police at Green Beach for transport by mike-boat out to the ship. The colonel consented to this.

Mangas offered to drive the lieutenant and Cazetti in his jeep. Cazetti sat in the back. They left at a crawl out of the compound and headed down the perimeter road.

"You're going too fast," Lieutenant Cercio said to Mangas.

Mangas said, "Sorry, sir. Sorry, Cazetti."

"Don't worry about being a private." The lieutenant turned around. "Nothing will change when you get back."

"Nobody was under me anyway, sir."

"That's right," said the lieutenant. "Here. You want a piece of gum?"

"That's okay, sir."

"I'll have one," Mangas said. They chewed gum.

Sunbeams flared on the windshield from the left as the sun burned over the range. Small-arms fire was crackling off in the Hooterville. On the right, they saw Second Platoon, Bravo moving out for patrol around checkpoint 76. Corporal Paugh and Doc Latour were walking abreast in the middle of the column. Doc heard the jeep driving down on them.

"Ve-hicle! From the rear!"

The platoon called, "HUH!"

Paugh and Doc split to either side of the road as Mangas brought the jeep creeping between them.

"One for the Air Force," Cazetti said to Paugh.

"You said that," Paugh said.

"How many roads, Doc?"

"The answer really blows, man," Doc said. "One."

Paugh started shouting, "Spread-em-out, port-arms-outboard." The jeep caught up with Lieutenant Irish at the point of the column. Cazetti saluted him confidentially.

The jeep went on. They perceived some more small-arms fire coming from the south, from Kaldeh, a road junction a few hundred yards beyond the southern tip of the perimeter.

Lieutenant Cercio said, "Mangas, stop the jeep. Let me get a look at this." Mangas stopped the jeep behind a rise of berms.

"Come on, Cazetti."

Cazetti followed the lieutenant out of the jeep and up the rise of the berm. They could see a traffic jam stalled on the coast road. Fumes floated upward from it. Cazetti saw the ships through the wavering fumes. Civilians stood outside their cars or sat on the cabs of trucks.

They were screening their eyes and looking towards the firefight, cheering at times, after sustained bursts of fire. Two tanks and a squad with Dragon missiles on their shoulders came down the perimeter road and passed Mangas's jeep to get nearer to the fire.

"I did all I could," Lieutenant Cercio said.

"I know," said Cazetti. They walked along the berm for a way.

"That's pretty good fire."

"Yes, sir."

"Twenty-nine and a wake-up is really all it is."

"The truth is I don't care," Cazetti said. "I want to go to the brig. I feel like it." He raised his soft-cover a little on his head and put his hands in his pockets. "And, on ship, I'll get you a copy of *Knocked-up Mamas*, sir."

"Excellent idea," the lieutenant said. "When you get back, we'll go to the club up in Junieh. We'll fix you up. Don't worry about it."

"Really, sir?" Rounds came cracking overhead.

"Doggone!" Mangas shouted. "Get down!"

Cazetti and the lieutenant dropped. They lay flat. The rounds stopped cracking and they zizzed low, some came sputtering into the berm. Mangas tore his rifle off the dashboard, locked in a magazine, and scrambled up the berm.

Lieutenant Cercio spun himself to face the fire, and to slide back down the safe side of the berm. A round caught him in the collarbone and tore out the back of a lung.

They pulled Lieutenant Cercio down off the berm. Cazetti shrugged him onto his shoulders and got his knee up over the back of the jeep and rolled the lieutenant onto the seat. This caused the lieutenant terrible pain. He gurgled a shriek from it. Mangas spun the jeep around. Rounds cracked over them, then faded behind them when they were speeding up the perimeter, passing the Mules and the Six-by's. Lieutenant Cercio was getting quieter.

The jeep got to the Battalion Headquarters building when there was a boxing smoker ongoing in front of the shower tents. Mangas ran for the corpsmen and they stretchered Lieutenant Cercio into the Aide Station. Mangas and Cazetti followed them inside. Yuck and Platt were lying there.

The Military Police came for Cazetti and took him on the mike-boat out to the ship. He showered the blood off there and pulled on clean utilities. He was put in the brig and he sat down on the bunk. He stayed sitting for a long time, and he thought about the lieutenant. Then he lay down. He refused to think of Philomena. Word came about Cercio. The lieutenant was stabilized in the Battalion Aide Station. He was flown to Larnaca, and then to Germany, and then nobody knew anymore.

He found he liked the brig. Cazetti looked at *Knocked-up Mamas* every day and tormented Cossaboom. The single bunk hung off the bulkhead from a pair of chains. The creamy paint was thick on the rivets and the bars. The brig was quiet, as it was deep in the hull under the waterline at the end of a passageway. The two adjacent cells were empty. Nobody came except for Cossaboom who sat at a field desk without, surrounded by mount-out boxes full of manila files. Cossaboom filed papers and drew papers from files, pressing beads of sweat off his round white head with his plump white hand. Cazetti was still in the brig when the Embassy was blown. A little news about it reached him there by way of Cossaboom.

The brig was opened up, in time, and Cazetti was floated ashore. He walked up the perimeter and stopped off to rest with Bravo. Cazetti sat down on a pallet in front of a bunker which had a stovepipe snaked out through the sandbags, pouring cook-smoke into the boughs of a spreading olive tree. The smoke bled out into a bright haze coming down from the hills. Inside the bunker the cooks were singing the "Duke of Earl." Cazetti heard the singing at his back through the sandbags and he looked at the sign-post of wooden arrows that was there, squinting his eyes in the haze:

DRUZE FORCES—1 KILOMETER
ISRAELI FORCES—600 METERS
AMAL FORCES—300 METERS
PLO REGULARS—200 METERS
MOURABITOUNE—LOOK BEHIND YOU
LIBYA—600 MILES
KATMANDU—7,900 MILES
PARMA, OHIO—7,900 MILES
DANANG—8,000 MILES
MUSTANG RANCH—9,500 MILES
DISNEYLAND—10,500 MILES

Ballory, the midget sniper, was on a berm, his elbow locked around his knee, with a small American flag on a short pole and a Marine Corps flag on a shorter pole sticking out of the packed clay on the top of the berm. The flags flapped and the strips of cloth from Ballory's helmet flapped and the sling of his Winchester bowed in the wind. The bright haze poured over the hills and permeated everything. The wind was carrying the rumble of artillery and the burning crackle of the firefights up on the hills. The ground had changed. Cazetti put his hand on it. Artillery concussions vibrated it. The scape of the hills in the arty duels and firefights above encircled the perimeter. Cazetti thanked Ballory for his magazine.

There were delays, in the military echelons, in assigning a replacement for Lieutenant Cercio, but a man was finally sent in during the very early days of the summer. On the tarmac at LZ Rock, a two-rotor chopper, in silhouette against the haze, dropped its nose with the rotors whirring. The tailgate unfolded and the hunched figure of a man dropped like an egg out the tail of a goose. He was sandy-haired, eyeglassed, thin-lipped, and slight. He carried a long cloth map case that was stenciled: USMC The Big Tubular One. Captain McLatchie walked through the rotor-wash. Davey stepped forward from the jeep with Cain and Cazetti.

"Captain McLatchie, sir. I'm Staff-Sergeant Davey."

"Greetings from 'Lant, Staff-Sergeant. Call me Captain Mac. You're going to do it anyway."

"This is Private Cazetti, your duty-flick."

"Combat photographer?"

"Yes, sir," Davey said. "A real one."

"Welcome aboard, Captain Mac," Cazetti said.

"Get this straight. I don't need to feel welcome. Is that clear?"

"Sure, sir."

"This is Sergeant Cain. Part of the Counter-Intell det," Davey said. Captain Mac popped his cheek with his tongue and nodded, looking at Cain. "Garces, the interrogator, is up at the COC."

"Let's go," said Captain Mac.

Captain Mac shook hands with the colonel in the main bay of the COC. The Lebanese oil stove was gone. Warm wind carried through the open barred window. The Intell crew settled in around the field desks inside the partition.

Garces stood plotting activity on the tac-maps with a long white cigarette bouncing on his lip.

"Garces," Davey said. "This is Lieutenant Cercio's replacement from 'Lant, Captain Mac."

Garces trayed his cigarette and offered his hand. "Captain . . . it's an honor."

"Sir," Davey said. "You want that Cain runs you down the Counter-Intell story first?"

"No. I want the intercepts from Radio Battalion, then gimme the tactical sits, then I'll hear Counter-Intell. Where's the message board?"

"Back in the comm-shack, sir."

"Send Cazetti for it."

"Oh, that's not his job, sir," Davey said. "He's not cleared. He just got busted."

"I will gladly oblige the captain," Garces said. He walked out.

"What does an uncleared private do for me?"

"He's in the field, sir."

"While I'm in charge, which I am right now," the captain turned to Cazetti, "you do no recon unless I okay it." He turned then to Davey. "Get him cleared."

"Anybody want a stick of gum?" asked Cain. No one spoke. Cain shrugged and put a stick of gum in his mouth. Captain Mac lifted Garces's cigarette out of the ashtray, snapped a short length of ashes into a peach can, which hissed in the juice, and he put his glasses on. He sat down to read a piece of traffic and smoke Garces's cigarette.

Cain and Cazetti raided a couple meals from the supply tent and started up a jeep. Cazetti sat at the wheel and Cain got in back with his shotgun. Garces and Davey swung around in another jeep. Captain Mac and Minovich got into the jeeps and they pulled away, pushed out the gates, and ran up the airport road past the mosque.

Captain Mac signaled for Cain to lock a shell into the shotgun. Cain did. Captain Mac yanked Cazetti's rifle off the dashboard.

"Gimme a clip."

"What, sir?"

"Give me a clip."

"Sir, that's my rifle."

"Just drive."

Cazetti handed over a magazine and the captain locked and loaded, then turned his head back to Cain.

"Take the windows. I've got the street."

Cain nodded and he winked at Cazetti in the side mirror. The captain torqued the sling on his arm and put the rifle barrel outboard.

"Sir," Cazetti said, his voice trying in the windspeed. "This attitude is going to make the Lebs nervous."

"Let them be nervous."

"What I mean, sir, is . . . it'll tempt them to try us out."

"They're going to try us out all right. Just drive."

"Sir, anything happens, I want my rifle back."

"You just follow Minovich's jeep."

"Sir . . ."

"Do what I say, goddammit."

It was dark when they got to the ATC club in Junieh. Music radiated from the pool. The paper lanterns glowed. Minovich and Davey and Garces got out of their jeep, tightened their blouses, took off their flak jackets, and pinched up their soft-covers. They grouped up at Cazetti's jeep.

"This is the place, Captain."

"That I deduced," Captain Mac said. "I don't know about this. I don't like it."

"It's safe, sir. You could say the place is on the payroll."

"Does the colonel know about this?"

"I don't know, sir. Hitman knows. It's all right, sir. Come on in."

Captain Mac stood out of the jeep and gave Cazetti his rifle back. "You two wait here."

"Sir, I'm allowed. One time Hitman brought me in himself," Cazetti said.

"Wait here."

Cain waited for them to walk through the arch in the fence, then he said, "Wait here? . . . No, Captain, *you* wait here. What a boot to the Root. I got business in there. He don't."

Cazetti said, "The Hitman needs to talk to him. I'm allowed in there. I'm supposed to be in there. Cercio was going to set me up."

"You, so what. I definitely got business in there. Hey, Cazetti, what's a nice thing to say to some girl in French? And not dirty . . . I mean a compliment. Mushy."

"You can say, 'You are beautiful as the day.' That means: You are as beautiful as the day is. . . . Or you can say, 'You ravish me.' it means: You are ravishing me."

"I like those. I like both of those." Cain said.

"Cain," Cazetti said. "Why are we showing suckers to the Lebs? I mean, *Mac* and *Garces* are in there."

"You want to know?" Cain asked. He unlocked the shell from his shotgun.

"Yeah. Tell me."

"It's a flutter. . . . Clear your rifle."

"What's a flutter?" Cazetti cleared his rifle. "What kind of a term is that?"

"It means, we bring in suckers, the casual way, and if they try to trim your suckers, or worm Intell out of them, you can't trust your contacts."

"Minovich wants to bring Camille back to the States and he doesn't know if he can trust her? Are you saying that?"

"Maybe I'm saying that. I don't trust Sardine. Do you?"

"Is there a reason you need to trust her, Cain? Have you been in the Tracs with Sardine? I'll kill you."

"Calm down. Maybe I'm not saying that. Maybe I'm saying, I just don't trust her, and I'd like your view."

"Yes. I trust her. But I'm disgusted with her. And I'm disgusted with you. Cercio's shot, I'm in the brig, you're in the Tracs with Sardine."

"Cazetti. Calm down. It was just opportunity."

Sardine and Camille walked out from the arch. They were dressed alike in leather jackets with square buckles on useless belts, and short red cotton skirts; their baubles were different, but they both had their hair pinned up in balls at the backs of their heads. They were bringing a bottle of scotch. Greetings were traded. Kisses were given on cheeks. Thanks were given for the bottle.

"So, let's speak French." Sardine said to Cazetti.

"No. I don't think so."

"I prefer English anyway," Camille said. "Who can propose a toast?"

"I can," said Cazetti. "To that godlike Adonis, Lieutenant Cercio. How's that, Sardine?"

"What is wrong with you? I thought you were a priest, because you fell in love at the convent. It was a very funny story."

"Who told you that?" Cazetti shouted. His lips made an oval and he stared at Sardine.

"It was just a story in Junieh," said Camille. "I'm sure it's not true."

"I wanted to confess my sins to you, Cazetti," Sardine said. "Do you know why? Because I wanted you to love them. And if not you, Cain."

"Oh, don't taunt him," Camille said. "She's being silly. It was just a story. I heard some things from the abbess, Dorothe. She's my friend, you see. And she's a friend of Joe Sfir. I'm sure it's just a story."

"This isn't cute," Cazetti said.

"Let's drink to the lieutenant anyway," Cain suggested.

"I was so worried for a time, about my poor lieutenant."

"How is he?" asked Camille.

Cain said, "He's going to be all right. He's probably home in the States by now."

"I would like a toast to America. I was almost on the plane to Kennedy Airport. Did Minovich tell you?"

"He told me," Cain said.

"I didn't hear. I was in the brig," said Cazetti.

"We applied for a visa," Camille said. "But it was lost in the explosion, along with a very dear girlfriend of mine."

"Yes," Sardine said. "And along with my jewelry which she borrowed. I won't be stupid like that again."

"Here's a toast to her and your jewelry," Cazetti said. He drank.

"Whose side are you on?" Sardine asked.

"Me? I wish I had a side to be on. If I find one, I'll tell you if we win."

"What is wrong with you?"

"Nothing is." Cazetti reached in his cargo pouch, unbuttoning the flap. "Here's your lousy *Knocked-up Mamas*." He gave her the book and sat on the hood of the jeep by himself. Sardine stood quietly, holding the book. She squeezed on the ball of hair at the back of her head.

"How do you like our new captain?" Cain asked.

"He is simply not at ease," Camille said. "One can tell. He's apprehensive."

"He said we have the honor to be one of the occasional tragedies of American history."

"Have you those, occasionally?" Camille asked.

"I guess so," Cain said. "Our general odds are short."

"Ah, yes. Your mathematic. Well, come to the apartment later if you can."

"Don't look for that, Camille. We're driving for that captain," Cain said.

"Goodnight then, Cain."

"Goodnight, Camille."

"Are you coming?" Camille asked Sardine.

"Yes," said Sardine. "Cain, say good night to Cazetti for me when he's finished sulking."

"Yes, and for me too," said Camille. "He really is rather sulking. Good night, again, Cain."

"Good night," Cain said. "And, Camille, thanks again for the bottle."

"It's nothing. . . . Oh, I thought it was only a story."

The sunlight came down from the hills. Heat rose wobbling from the sand. Tar was melted on the roads. The muezzin called from the mosque. Nothing moved but the flies. It was the middle of the summer. It was hot.

There was a short diving screeching and two rockets exploded. Eyes opened in the COC. There was another screech and another impact. The field phones were spinning off like fishing reels. The scramble blurred for the helmets and flak jackets and weapons.

The field-phone voice came over, "This is MSSG. We're taking rockets. Hot right now. I say again: We've got incoming."

"Captain Mac, sir. MSSG taking rounds."

"Where's it coming in from?"

"Sir, don't know."

"Hit the goddamn holes."

They ran out from the COC while the rockets came in at intervals. Dirt fluttered from the thrash in the holes. The hollow pop of the rocket tubes somewhere made a whumping sound that bore down screeching and crashed into the ground with smoke and shrapnel spray.

A black lieutenant lifted his head from a lump of sandbag with his chinstrap tucked in his teeth. His face was dappled by shade where the sandy ground jagged around him. A screech bore down again.

"That's walking in behind us. Check your weapons. Check your weapons. Radio the FSC." He ducked. He reappeared. "Smokin'! . . . Who's got a smoke?"

Mangas fumbled out a pack of Marlboros. He took one in his quaking lips. He gave one to Cazetti. He then threw it back to the black lieutenant. The black lieutenant ducked. The red pack tumbled in an arching flight from one hole to another, where any hand reached up to get it in, and pull from it, and throw it on.

"This. My friend," Mangas said, "it was not like this before."

The whump in the haze sent the screeches of the rockets in. They pressed into the sand and the sand began to coat them. Sweat came out from hands and fingers, sand scratched in the rifle parts, the radio and shouting got muffled in the helmets underground. The hole was filled with crunched-up angry faces reckoning the seconds from the pop of the enemy tubes.

Cicchelero and the sergeant-major each had an arm around the other's neck.

"Did you take rockets in the Nam?" Cicchelero asked.

The sergeant-major made a bull toss with his head. "You bet."

"How many?"

"A whole bunch."

"Yo, I won't die like this, though, right?"

"Don't try anything hasty, because you sure could, young man. And I could too. You just get through it. You just get through it with your balls."

The flight-rip of another rocket cut the words the sergeant-major said. There was a salvo suddenly of six tubes popping off. Coming in, they struck the runways, and the shrapnel scraped the tarmacs and ripped with clanging into the metal sides of the hangar buildings.

In the burrow of the dirt was the counting, calling:

"Nother-one, one, two three. Down."

"Nother-one, one, two three. Down."

"Stay down."

"Down."

"It's what sergeant-major said. The sergeant-major."

After a time like this there was a lull. Lebanese troops pulled out from the runways in a column of armored machines. The rumble of the iron caterpillar treads and the shouting of the troops made a good sound. The word was spread between the holes that Radio Battalion had gotten an intercept that meant there would be more fire coming in momentarily. Magazines were pulled and tapped on the helmets. A firefight popped in the Hooterville. The sound of it went rising and it thickened. A major in the adjunct hole began to whistle "Green-Go the Rushers." More cigarettes smoked.

"Sir, please stop that." Cazetti said.

Mangas said, "I hate this. What's going on?"

"I don't know . . . sir, can you stop that?"

Neale ran along the building edge.

"A captain kicked me out of a hole. Can I get in your hole?"

"What?" said the sergeant-major.

"No lie. He said it was too crowded. Can you believe the man?"

"Goddamn foxhole's just like a Six-by. There's always room for one more."

"Get in," Cazetti said. "I'm getting out."

Cazetti pushed up with his arms out of the hole.

"Get back!" yelled the sergeant-major.

Cazetti rolled over his elbow on the ground and ran along the building. He was thinking of the Tracs. He was thinking of the thickness of the metal they were made of, and the big machine guns they had in the cupolas, and how they were parked in the shadow of the great Battalion Headquarters building, and he was motivated to run for them.

He was running between the nests of wire around the generators. A whistle coursed overhead. He could see the terminal building at the airport, and a white car racing towards it. He dove to the ground on his chest. A rocket hit ten meters from a sandbagged guard post on the perimeter. Shrapnel sprayed in a pink burst in the daylight and the splinters stunned sandbags of the post. He could see a Trac, but he couldn't reach it. He lay flat around the wire with his cheek in the dirt. He breathed in dirt and coughed. Rockets flew into the runway hangars, and they hit on the airport road.

Time cleared, and the incoming ceased. Cazetti walked out to the road. The white car which raced had been stopped by a rocket and blown. The roof was torn off. There was smoke from the twists of metal, and only particles of the driver remained.

They were called to dig and enlarge the holes, making them deeper and wider, laying roofs of aluminum airstrip decking over the parapets. They were interrupted by incoming, and they hunched in the holes they were dressing, and time cleared, and they rose to dig again.

Blouses came off and headbands were tied. Bared arms worked from the flak jackets. A one-rotor helo came flapping over the compound. Cicchelero looked up at it.

"You know what I wish I was? A crew chief on a Huey."

"Don't you want some glory, Chick? Come on, man, bag that sand," said Neale. "Think of yourself as a master craftsman, a sandominium lord. Think of yourself on the cover of *Sand Home*

Magazine. You're awesome, Chick, I swear to God. I swear. You're a Marine."

"Get out. But I am a master craftsman."

The Lebanese in the armored column had been resisted in the Hooterville and the air was pulsing with the firing clash.

Davey crouched at the hole which Cazetti and Mangas were opening, "I remember this from Khe-Sahn." He offered his canteen. Mangas took it, the water lurching down his throat. "The first day Charlie opened up with seven hundred rounds."

"This sucks, Davey," Cazetti said. He took a drink.

"I know it, bud. I know it does. Is there something I can do?"

"Get me to that poz back up in Alayah. Talk to Minovich. Talk to Hitman."

"I'm just being gentle with you, bud. I can't do a thing."

"This sucks."

"I know it does. But don't think about what can happen to you. Think of what could happen to me! That tattoo. Listen, nobody lied to you. You understand me? This is what the Suck's about. There's nothing better to tell you. For general odds in the Nam you could lose one man in forty, but, sometimes, you get a situation around a unit and it drops under ten. You just do sometimes. Our mathematic took a dive. Look out about your moves from here on in, bud."

He took his canteen back, and turned on the balls of his feet. He went back into the COC.

The pings from the entrenching tools mingled in the heat with the rotor-chop, and the radio squawk, and the uptown fire in the city. Artillery on the hills was bursting in pillars of ash-white smoke. Fatigue was setting in and they flopped, more or less, in the bunkers when the rounds came in again. Nearby a tube stung out.

"That's outgoing. One tube, gents. Illumination round dropping on the target. It says 'We got you, Rags.'"

It quieted things down. The afternoon sun was settling on the rim of the sea. The digging and the bagging continued in the hour and the sandominiums were made.

The day ended. The muezzin called from the speakers at the mosque. The diggers were gathered around the sandbag walls before the doors to the COC. The colonel came. He had his helmet in his hand. Cain was standing behind him with Captain Mac. All the diggers were standing drowned in sweat, leaning on their tools. Some were jacketed, some were bare-backed with soaked green bandages crowning their heads. All the faces were taut and serious. The colonel scraped at his hair stubble with his fingers and he looked around the crowd. Everyone was silent.

"Interesting day."

"Yes, sir."

"Yes, sir." A couple of heads cocked to the side. Cicchelero took his headband and wiped out his armpits.

"It's a fearsome thing. You better believe it is. . . . Now, some of you are thinking that you've seen the world come down, that you are done with what we have to do. Well, you have not begun. You're going to need the nerve you showed me here today. I know you have it. I am proud of you. Corporal Neale, open the bar."

A doubtful cheer rose.

The light was cast with a purple lilt and bats flew out from blasted pockets of the building. Rich green leaves of a locust tree entered through a hole and scratched against the wall as a wind moved them. Cazetti was climbing up a stairs. He dropped his gear on the flat of the roof after climbing up an iron ladder. He moved his head to look at the sea where the ships were tracing the coastline. Fumes rose from their funnels. On the range, the sunset rays were catching glass on the faces of a few low structures and golden blazes shined from these. The city lulled.

Minovich had vodka. He was standing, swigging it, and it pearled in the light through the glass. Cain was hunched over his knees with his back against the parapet.

"The diplomats won't deal, but they made the paperwork," said Minovich. "I can get her out, but only if I marry her."

"How many days have we got left? I mean, before the Root goes down?" Cain asked.

"Ten or so. Who knows? The captain gives it ten."

"Mac?" Cazetti asked.

"He's a freak," said Cain. "But he got the target. I was there. He shuffled it out of a hundred grids. It was magic. It was like intuitive. He was on those guns like a wasp."

Cazetti said, "I guess you lived to talk about it. . . . Let me pull on that." He grabbed the bottle and sat down on the parapet.

Minovich pinched his Skoal. He looked at Cain. "If I go ahead and do it, you're there. Am I right?"

"Yeah. If you can do it. You don't have much time."

"Imagine that I know that," Minovich said. "If I can get to Joe Sfir or the Hitman, I can pull it off."

"Before the Root goes down."

"I know what I'm aiming at, for chrissake, Cain."

"You can get her out?" Cazetti asked. "Get me out too, if you're going to the trouble."

"Don't make a joke, Cazetti," Cain said.

"What joke? If you're pulling people out of Lebanon, I'd like to sign up for that. Where do I sign up?"

"We're stuck in it, Cazetti," Minovich said. "What I've got is a window of opportunity, and that's all. Ten days from now, it'll be hard. Hard. That's what."

"He's going to do it," said Cain. He liked that. "Okay, Gunner, listen. I'm in. I'm there."

"Can I go too?" Cazetti asked.

"You want to go?"

"What do you think?"

"I think it's fair. Cazetti's been okay," Cain said. "He's been secure ever since the brig."

"I wouldn't even want to go without Cazetti," Minovich said. "He's a priest. At least, I heard."

"From who?" Cazetti tensed.

"I got it from a contact. Let's go and find the Hitman."

They drove out in the morning with the Counter-Intell jeep. They loaded up and locked. The traffic swirled around them and there were jams around the camps. Around the pump-spouts of the water wells there were women lining up with vessels.

They parked the jeep at the club in Junieh and boarded Joe Sfir's car, packing it, and laps were used as seats. They left Junieh and came up a mountain road under Phalange control. The day was pretty and light peeked through the cedar boughs.

It was all a little rushed. There was the glow of holy vigil lamps on the joints of the iconostasis. Small-arms fire was distant, but it leaked into the chapel. The priest stood still and he was silent. He had a robe embroidered with white flowers and a cross on his back was gold. It was silk and had a cincture at the hip. Nuns were ringed around him, kneeling in their habits with their faces stiff under the white cake canisters that crowned their heads.

The old nun rose and signaled to the priest. He approached them one by one. They stood to receive communion. The priest held a plate under the chin when the mouths opened. Philomena stood up. She opened her mouth.

Minovich was kneeling and next to him Camille was kneeling too. On Minovich's side Cain was standing, and Sardine stood next to Camille. They didn't move and they received communion in that way.

In back of them were the Hitman and Cazetti and Joe Sfir. The priest came around to them. It was quiet and the robe made a rustling sound.

The priest rubbed out his vessels and folded his napkin up. The nuns sang something briefly. They sang in French.

"Set me as a seal upon thy heart,
as a seal upon thine arm,
for love is strong as death.
Jealousy is cruel as the grave,
Her shafts are shafts of fire,
even the flames thereof."

It was pretty.

It all had to be done in a hurry. Cazetti went up to the tower with a radio in his hand. He pulled on Philomena's sleeve with the other going up the tower stairs. They sat down.

"You press this. That makes a tone burst," Cazetti said. Philomena looked on with a finger sideways at the base of her nose. "That sound is a tone burst. That's the encryption. It's secure."

"That sound is pretty."

"After the tone burst, you can speak. First you ask for us. We are 'Hitman.' Hitman, Hitman. Say that."

"Very well, Hitman."

"Then you identify yourself with a code name. What code name do you want?"

Philomena thought. *"Vierge-Marie!"*

"No!" Cazetti said, "No, no. Are you being stupid?"

"Then, Pacifico?"

"Okay. No one can know you have this radio. That is very serious. You never use it, except in extreme danger. Hitman will help you. Do you understand? If you call us, you must be ready to leave."

Philomena thought. "Perhaps we are old enough for martyrs now."

"No you are not. That's why this radio."

"Well, it is more prudent. That's true. What joy to see you receive the communion of Our Lord. I thought, Our Lady sent me to fetch you by the ear. Like that. You are my brother."

Cazetti grew impatient with her. "If you want. Listen to me. You are as beautiful as the day."

Philomena laughed. "Not this again. I am not beautiful. And, what's more, I have something wrong with my body. It's worrying the doctor. It's like a scoliosis, but it's multiple."

"What are you saying? Multiple sclerosis? Is that what you want to say?"

"Yes. That's it. And that's not so pretty, is it? No, Our Lady is the one who is beautiful. I am a nun. I am your sister."

"Wait. Shut up. Listen to me. Why don't you understand? You ravish me. Do you understand? You don't want to. Okay, it's not your intention. But that is what you do. You ravish me. If you're crippled like the hand of Kalil, I don't even care. I can walk. That's all I do."

"You're being stupid. I do nothing but pray for you."

"I don't care."

"Don't look at me like that. It's like a wolf. It's stupid. I don't like that." She crossed herself.

Cazetti grabbed her arm. "Stop. You leave this place. You marry me. It's like that."

"What stupidity! I am already married. I'm a nun. I am married to Christ. The idea that you just said is completely repulsive. It's repugnant. It's adultery. That repels me."

"Would you listen!"

"No. It's impossible."

She bolted down the stairway and took a door into a corridor. Cazetti chased her into a refectory. There was a long table in there. She took one end of it. She pointed with her finger to the other end of it.

"There," she said. "I can scream. I know how to do that."

Cazetti stood at the curve of the table's farther end. Philomena touched her head with the palms of both her hands.

"There is something inside of you that is not pure. It is not yet pure. I will pray," she said.

"There is something inside of you too, that is not pure."

"Yes, that's true. I didn't say I was pure."

"I don't want for you to be. I want you with me."

"Where? To do what?" she asked.

"I don't know."

"Of course not, because it's impossible. You don't understand. God, you're stupid."

"Yes. That is your fault. You make me stupid. I don't even think. I can't distinguish anything from anything. Because I love you."

She put her fingers over her eyes, and then looked at Cazetti again. "You cannot. It's not done because Our Lord is jealous. You cannot ask this of me. It is a very great sin. But if you love me, do not test my heart, or we will not live, neither you nor me to see the snow at

Christmas. Now: I will never see you again. I will never speak to you again. I will not pray for you anymore. I will ask another sister to do it. Wait."

She turned past a crucifix on the wall and walked into a pantry. Cazetti slumped forward and held himself up from the table with his arms locked. She returned with a dark, spoiling sprig of mint leaves and a bruised pear, which she gave to him.

She left him. Cazetti ate the mint and the pear.

Joe Sfir arranged for two bridled donkeys to be waiting for the Minoviches when the car got back to the ATC in Junieh. There were flowers in the bridles. The Minoviches rode them from the entry to the pool side, and they held hands. Minovich carried Camille through the arch. That was the end of the ceremony.

At the tables on the porch there were glasses with champagne in them and bottles of it waiting in buckets on stands. There were fried pastry morsels. There was music playing. Hitman gave Minovich an envelope, and everyone knew there was money inside.

The talk at the table was about PanAm jets and how many days were left before there would be no going. It was decided Camille would go out in two days on a route through Paris. The couple looked happy and it was a pretty occasion, but everything was being softened by an uncomfortable amount of spontaneous reassurances, and there was a doubtful grain to the talk. The champagne did not mollify it. Cain and Sardine held hands in the open, and it made Hitman and Cazetti scowl. Sardine tried to distract the table, to prompt for amusement by pointing with her champagne glass at Cazetti and saying, "Well, I see it was not just a story. Who would have dreamed of it?" But there was no amusement for the table in the story of Cazetti and Philomena. It tended to point to the difficulties at hand, the way the mathematic did.

Minovich stayed in Junieh that night with Camille in her apartment. Hitman, Cain, and Cazetti drove back through town and got to the lines and the compound after dark when fires were burning in the downtown grids, pulsing from the blacked-out towers. Sardine came down in a French adjutant-major's car later and, when he had gone back to the Hippodrome, she ducked into one of the amphibious assault vehicles with Cain.

IV

In the City of Incoming

THERE WAS A helmet cover ashore that said: Rubble Rat.

There was a far siren whine, a great pressing stream of traffic moving for the airport. Planes took off with lines of people standing in the aisles. In the Sabra and Shatila camps, the multiplex tire stacks and junk piles changed and the lines of women storing water were long.

Downtown on Hamra Street there was no traffic. There were only two people, a man and a boy, eating at the open cafe. A vendor pushed his cart toward the corniche. There were a few trees, and a few hanging lights on the boulevards tossed in the wind.

Then there was a kind of Intell dinner that Hitman arranged for, near the St. George's Hotel and hulk of the embassy. All the Intell crew sat down at a refectory table. The room was dark with wood paneling and candles. There were no other customers. The waiters and the maitre d' were looking afraid. The maitre d' was smiling, rubbing his hands. The barman shook. The more the night wore on, the worse they looked afraid. Davey threw his arms around Cazetti's neck and gouged his head with his knuckles. The noogies didn't help a thing. It was coming.

Fed and bowlegged, they walked out of the restaurant smoking cigars in a huddle. The blacked-out destruction surrounded them. Now and then, from a shattered window, a light shined out. A prostitute rushed into a darkened doorway. They went into the jeeps and passed through a roadblock. Captain Mac copped a slouch and flipped the finger to the Lebs. The jeep traced down the corniche with no sounds to muffle the crash of the surf against the breakwater, under the yellow lights on the deserted roadway, passing the blown Embassy, the blown hotels and hospitals, the squalid camps, the breathless city.

Neale used the butt of his rifle to bunt the tennis ball that Mangas threw to him. Mangas caught it in his thighs. Cicchelero laughed. They were at the jeep park outside the COC. Mangas was winding up another underhanded pitch.

"Wait, man," Neale said. The little cleaning tool locker in the rifle butt had come open. Neale was pushing the cleaning rods back up into the stock.

Small-arms fire began ripping in the Hooterville. The volume expanded and the direction of the fire shifted. A rocket grenade exploded. Neale turned towards the fire, with the muzzle of the rifle pointed behind him. Cazetti hopped off the hood of a jeep. He put his hand on Neale's back. They stood still.

Neale said, "That's close-up, man."

A net of rounds in a swarm cracked over their heads and there were ricochets off the building and ticks in the trunks of the trees. They scrambled for their gear and the holes. Cicchelero crouched behind the sandbag wall in front of the bar while the fire thickened and the angle lowered. Neale ran hunched into the COC and Cazetti ran in with him to grab his bandoleer.

A boot-lieutenant with his pistol drawn was crouched under a table. Cazetti ducked into the partition of the -2.

Davey shouted over the fire, zipping up his flak jacket. "Okay, bud, hold them and squeeze them. Drop them when you see them. Get a hole and do the job. Do it."

"Davey—I'm not ready for this."

"No choice, bud. Go!"

Cazetti pulled his head through the sling of the bandoleer and moved. Rounds were hitting the outside of the building. The colonel pulled the boot-lieutenant out from under the table. Radios and field phones made a buzz-storm, and Neale was on one of the radios, and his eyes, under the helmet, looked large and they glimmered.

Cazetti didn't like the bunkers at the front of the COC. They had no field of fire. He kept as low as he could to the mazes of sandbag walls and moved behind the COC to the foxholes near the generators and the rolls of concertina wire. Concrete chips were splintering off the COC building. The blasts of mortars and rocketed grenades crashed down with the fire, leaping through the air from the east. Over the wire rolls a red light burst, and shrapnel ripped in the treetops and stunned the box metal of the generators.

In the foxholes there, rifle muzzles moved over the ground in the arms of the hunkered-down figures like the bows of violins. Magazines were tapped on the helmets and there was the crush-lock sound of the bolts going home in the weapons.

Cazetti rolled into an empty foxhole. He squared off his helmet. Looking left over his shoulder, he saw that Yuck was in a hole behind him, shivering, with a dopey leer on his face.

"Now you got your goozler in a fix, ain'tcha boy?"

"Shut up and throw a smoke."

Yuck threw a pack of Marlboros that didn't make it to Cazetti. Cazetti hurled his back against the lip of the hole and reached for the pack, keeping his eyes outboard towards the line of burned-out buses. He got the pack and drew one out, and lit up shaking. The black lieutenant moved up hunched on his knees with a loop of bandoleers over his shoulder, yelling over the fire and the churning hum-roar of the generators.

"You need any rounds?"

"I'll take a bandoleer," Cazetti shouted.

"Look for feet moving under those buses. If you see any feet, let fly."

"Shoot the feet, sir?"

"It's bad, but it's all we got."

"Sir, I'm gone."

Cazetti pushed up and ran crouching past the generators to a vegetated area at the latrine where there were two trunks of fallen palm trees. The tree trunks sat on a rise above the road that ran down to the Battalion. He could look across the runways, and up the hills at the base of the range, and, on the rooftop of a building rising to his left front, there was a team with a machine gun. The forward field around the mortars at Bravo Company was spotted with white artillery bursts. The Hooterville was speckled with muzzle flashes in a lowering dark green light. The machine-gun crew opened up from the rooftop. A tank came grumbling up the road from the Battalion with its gun barrel directed at the hills. It was followed by a Trac. The great metallic clanking of the treads overcame the rasping of the fire for a moment. When the armor had passed, Cazetti saw two rocketed grenades launch out of tubes from the Hooterville olive grove. They crossed in their oncoming flight and impacted at Bravo Company, landing in a tent, blowing the tent into flying wings of canvas and shrapnel cinders.

The machine gun on the rooftop continued to beat out its fire. Rounds started whizzing and ticking into the brush and the tree trunks, and Cazetti knew that a set of small-arms had laid target on him. He peered over the trunk to spot the muzzle flashes. He could not pick any out from all the sparking sieve of fire. He thumbed the switch to automatic and triggered out a magazine in three bursts of whacking fire, while the rifle jumped. He locked in another magazine. He considered, then, his range, and reckoned he was only popping rounds into the back of Bravo Company lines. He needed to get outboard. Rounds continued with their snacking at him. He hated and hated the day. He jumped and made a run. Rounds flew ahead of him. And he ran in his gear, in a jangling ball of cloth and harness, over the wire, the fires, and the foxholes with a dark green vision, the aquarium-water vision of terror.

Ahead of him he saw the air-struck building which rose over the cellar they were berthing in. He reeled into there, pulling forward with his left shoulder, and he gripped the corner of a concrete wall and breathed directly into it until he had his wind again and could begin again to think a little. "Penetrated. Overrun. Hand-to-hand at night." Altogether, such, his thoughts. The small-arms rounds were pocking up the building. The weird warbling tones from the speakers at the mosque were starting. He held his breath and cut around a near interior corner, keeping his back slammed against the concrete;

and so he moved, from wall to wall through the darkened rooms and corridors. He heard the missing step of feet and a knocking crunch on rubble. From a room full of ashes which spilled onto the corridor floor, a head and a rifle asserted more and more until the wedge of a face with an eye looking out of it came gently into view.

"Yo. Take it easy."

"Cicchelero?"

"Yeah. Yo. Take it easy."

"Okay."

"I got a piece of mortar in my leg."

"Hold on."

Cazetti pushed down along the corridor wall until he came nose to nose with Cicchelero.

"Come on. We'll get out to the bunker at the back. Look up the airport road. Can you walk?"

"Yeah, but, I walk no good."

Cazetti helped him hobble out the corridor and step up, out a blasted hole in the building side. They put down in a slit trench which faced the iron spears of fence on the perimeter. They could look out long down the airport road. The road looked long out into darkness to the city, crackling and glowing out of pools of orange firelight. A web of tracers arched from the Hooterville.

Cazetti unpouched a bandage from the medical kit on his war-belt back. This made him think of Philomena.

"Chick, get on your side."

Cicchelero did. Cazetti unsheathed his bayonet and cut up the back of Cicchelero's trouser leg, sopped with blood. A thumb-sized piece of shrapnel had gone deep into the hamstring and Cazetti could only see the spiky edge of it.

"Am I supposed to dig it out?"

"Yo. Don't dig it out."

"I'll bandage it."

"Okay."

Cazetti tore at the plastic wrap with his teeth, and stuck the flat of it against the wound, and turned the sticking tapes around the hairy leg.

"What's up with this? I mean it. Yo. What's up with this?"

"The Root is going down. That's all I know. What can I say to you? It sucks. It's bad. That's all I know."

Cicchelero stayed lying on his side inside the trench. Cazetti looked outboard through the fence spears while the ground mumbled with concussions of artillery and the nets of fire spread out across the city. The darkness covered the area morbidly.

The first light was glowing off the range of the

mountains in the east. The endless pulse of fire had not diminished. At a turn inside the trench, a mouse was chewing on a packet of instant cocoa powder.

"I like mice," Cicchelero said. "Yo, they amuse me."

Cazetti could not see any bodies moving on the road or in the windows of any of the buildings. Battalion grunts in the guard-post hooches were held still inside the hooches. There were no targets outboard. There was only the sound of the steady sheets of fire, close and far, a haze of cordite and the cordite smell, and a low relentless hum from the generators grinding.

"Where is everybody?"

"That's what I wonder too."

"They could be back in the building."

"Maybe, I guess."

"You need attention. We could find a corpsman. I'll help you walk. Come on."

They came into the building through the blasted hole and they hobbled to the stairs that went down to the cellar. There was a fire team spread down the steps. They all looked up at Cicchelero and Cazetti. Rounds popped down the corridor with stony echoes.

They handed Cicchelero down from one man

to the next. Neale and Mangas were at the bottom of the stairs and looking up.

"Where've you been, man?" Neale asked.

"In a mouse hole with Chick. What's this?"

"We call it Death Squad, my friend," Mangas said. "If we get penetrated, they buzz us on the field phone, and we engage. You're deputized a member."

"Let me tell you, that, I love."

They waited on the stairs for the clicking of the field phone. The air was hot and the gear made it hotter, while the fire popping on the building picked off flinders. They waited and smoked and sweat poured off their faces into pools on the steps. The blouses and the jackets were soaked and dark with sweat. They tied their heads with bandages but this did no good. The nose tips and the chins sweat streamingly. The Armed Forces radio was playing from the cellar.

There was a whumping from a tube. It was close, loud cannon fire.

"Arty. Outgoing. Ours," Cazetti said. The eyes on the stairs were dreadful and bared.

The field phone began spinning out its clicks. Heads dropped. Helmets came on. Bolts went home in the rifles.

Neale put the field phone down.

"Unlock. They're just letting us know the story. The One-niner-eights popped illumination on a target. If there is another round, the rounds will be H.E. Get your dicks hard, gentlemen," Neale said. "Because H.E is high explosive. And high explosive is killing, man. And killing is coming down."

On the stairs they unlocked and smoked and dripped. Everyone was silent for a span. They listened to the singing on the radio. Then there came the sound, the great scumping noise of the outgoing full battery salvo.

A cheer went up with backslapping and hoots. A chant was invented and thickened up with voices, "H.E. H.E. H.E. H.E. One-niner-eights." It was as if some god had spoken.

The radio was tuned up loud. A Puerto Rican lance-corporal who was crouching misty eyed on the stairs, with a piece of his nose torn off, but no longer bleeding, said, "Sonny and Cher, man. When they broke up, man, it shocked the nation. It shocked the nation. Man, it did."

The sergeant-major, from above, jostled through the bodies, touching shoulders as he moved down the steps. He removed his helmet when he got the bottom, standing in the cellar.

"Gather around here."

Everybody circled him.

"Hey, Sergeant-Major. What's the *story* topside? What the hell is *up*?"

"Fair for you to ask, young man," the sergeant-major said. "Well. We got a couple KIA and wounded men all over since last night. All the line companies are engaged. We just laid a full battery salvo on some Druze guns. It knocked them out. That was motivating fire, gents. You want to know: Is it bad? I say: Affirmative. Is it going to get any worse? I say: Roger to that. This is what we do for a living, gentlemen. Do you roger?"

"When do we pull out of this?" Cazetti asked.

"We don't pull out. We're hanging fire. This is rock and roll."

"We got the low ground. Our backs are to the sea. We're surrounded by a built-up area full of enemy. What are we *supposed* to roger?" Neale asked.

"I don't know, son. Stand by."

The field phone clicked, Neale answered it.

"Cazetti."

Cazetti grabbed the handset. Cain's voice was on the line, and the sound of the topside fire. "Go ahead, Cain."

"Can you get up?"

"Yeah."

"Then get up here."

"How's it look?"

"It looks not good. We're holding fine-okay though."

Cazetti came out of the building, ran across the line of buses in the compound, worked into the sandbag mazes, and got into the COC.

Cain, Garces, Captain Mac, and Davey were at task with the tac-maps and the field phones. The outboard elements called in movements and positions, which the Intell crew assessed and marked, and they supplied the air and artillery support coordinators with the enemy targets to be struck.

On the field desk where Cain was crouched with two field phones at his ears, Cazetti saw a stack of yellow message slips.

"Target cards?"

Cain yelled into a phone, "The radar's working on it. We'll check it out with radar. Hold up. Stay on the line." He leaned his head and winced to bring Cazetti nearer, "You got about six hundred targets in that stack of cards. Plot them on the map. The checkpoints between the perimeter and Alpha Company out at the University were hit early this morning. They're all cut off. Thirty-five got hit with anti-aircraft fire. Sixty-nine is rolling Amal bodies out of the way with the machine gun." He pointed to his left-side phone, "Bravo Company thinks they're getting hit from tubes up in Alayah."

Garces said, "The Battery took out three tubes of Druze, five trucks, a spotter counts up fifteen dead. That Battery is motivated. Look at this." He showed Cazetti a Radio Battalion intercept. It said, "Radio Bn. Intercept: Israeli spotter reports—Yanks fire is OK."

In time it was growing dark again, and while the dark lowered, there was a lull. Smoke was rising from the city.

Prayers were calling out from the mosque.

There were hollow laugh-echoes in the cellar. Mangas sat with Neale in a rectangular dead-end space where there were candles lit. Mangas sat on an ammo can. They were looking at the candles. Neale opened a can of mushrooms broiled in butter. They looked at Cazetti walking in and looked back at the candles.

Neale spoke slowly, staring. "I told Mangas, man, last night, in the COC, I looked at Cazetti. I said, we're gonna die. I said, grab onto your balls, boys, we're gonna die."

"What do you know from Intell?" Mangas asked, "Who's doggone hitting us?"

"Everyone."

"Yeah?"

"Syrians, PLO, Amal, Druze, Mourabitoune. The Phalange hit too. I don't know why."

"Man, I'm telling you, there's nothing we can do for these people, except rape their women and shoot their combat."

"The Israelis are pulling back to the Awali River. That will not help. On the other side of the range, there are big numbers of gooners. Syrians, PLO, and they've got tanks. They can come down a road from Alayah. Joe Sfir and the Phalange are there waiting for it."

"That's not the worst part, man," Neale said.

"What is?" Mangas asked.

"Cicchelero won a Purple Heart."

Day after day, a radio played. There was fire and artillery and the COC cranking up. Sirens and guitars and the sound of lungs, and the beat-out of machine guns. A coil of razor wire, the tin cans of beer, a pile of cargo, choppers coming in to LZ Rock to medevac the wounded and the dead. Mortars on the runway. And fire and the COC cranking up. And time moved in the maps, in the ships, in the turrets, in the cross-hairs, the cellar going dark with the Death Squad on the stairs. A piece of armor smoking on the line, and a helo whapping over the beach victorious. But there was something so unclear, so nuclear, and worse at night, under the moonlight and the starlight with the hills wrapped up in purple vapor, and a bony gleam on the curls of the wire and shadows under cammy-nets. In the nightscopes from the trenches and parapets, the scenes moved like ashes sliding in a wired eye and the kafiyahs of the gunmen slid across rooftops and windows with a motion that was blinking, and then downed in the fire of the salted building.

Ashore there was a helmet cover:

SUICIDE SUNDAY 2 KIA 17 WIA
MORTAR MONDAY 3 WIA
TUBE-POP TUESDAY 1 KIA 5 WIA
WEDNESDAY MEDEVACS
ARTY THURSDAY 1 KIA 2 WIA
FRIDAY FISH
ISRAELI SATURDAY NIGHT

The Israeli headlights made a stream of silver beads snaking down the Sidon road on their way to the Awali River. It was a morning when the pulsing light of Venus spied over the range, and soon there were the parapets and holes again, and the fields burning when the rounds came in, when the *one, two-two* concussions twinged the ground, gapping the sandbags, the sand running out in ponytail streams under the stun of the shrapnel, and a radio played, day after day.

Time moved through, wandering the city of the incoming, visiting blown fruit stands and the Ice House and the Hippodrome, stopping at the lanyards of artillery on battery hills, and at a radio-det explosion where a Six-by crashed and a firefight popped up behind the red and white striped circus tent at the Italian camp. Time sucked in its navel and lay down in a hangar and looked up at the dusty poles of light in the shot-out roof, while the big stuff fell into the runway and concussions torqued the concrete, and Time flapped on its back like a fish. Time took a breath and dove into the tunnels that connected the Sabra and Shatila camps. It surfaced again loaded down with weapons and flung out its arms around the perimeter, to cut off certain elements, to lay siege on its tender flanks, and smirk at it with its slow eye.

And Time came in the COC, and vanished.

Captain Mac snapped around the partition and jabbed with his finger at the tac-maps on the wall. It was night. The field phones poured, and there was intense confusion and fury with incoming, and mayhem in parallel.

"There *are* guns in Alayah . . ." Captain Mac began.

"The radar don't turn a grid there, sir," said Davey.

"Get a man topside," the colonel said. "Plot that grid by muzzle flash. Get me that grid to fire."

"Spyglass—Spyglass," Davey said. "See if you can plot a muzzle flash. Look up in Alayah."

"Grid square thirty-six, forty-one," Cazetti said to Davey. "Ballory says erase it. The whole thing. It just took a hundred rounds of the big stuff."

A screech came in, and then a blast, a voice was calling: "WO-AH!" The light bulb spun from the ceiling.

Captain Mac spoke to the colonel. "That's a gun in Alayah, sir. That's where it has to be. The radar's not tracking a trajectory. It comes right down straight like a piss-ray."

"Get a muzzle flash and plot a grid," the colonel said. "Any goddamn day."

"Whiskey-Six is taking rounds, sir," Davey said. "Requests the Battery hit the grid. The mortars can't knock it out."

"Negative," the colonel said. "Finish the mission with mortars."

"Bravo Company is taking arty," Garces said. "Wadi-Shur; three tubes just went hot."

The colonel held a target card, and showed it to Captain Mac. "Check that grid. What's on it?"

The captain checked. "There's an orphanage, Colonel."

"Orphanage my ass. Fire the grid. . . . As you were, let the Navy fire that."

"Spyglass—Spyglass," Davey said. "Plot that tube. Plot that tube. Get your ass a muzzle flash."

A runner from Radio Battalion came in with an intercept folded in his hand. He handed it to Captain Mac.

"There's a mechanized gun firing on checkpoint 69," Cazetti said. "Sixty-nine requests the Cobras to engage."

"Affirmative," the colonel said. "Engage with air."

Another round of artillery doused the generated light for a moment. The same voice cried, "WO-AH!" The light sputtered on again. Captain Mac read the intercept squinting through his glasses. He looked up and he was furious.

"What is this, Cazetti? You come here. Now!"

Cazetti dropped his field phones and moved to the captain's desk behind a wall of mount-out boxes.

"Look at this. What is this?" Captain Mac read it out loud and held it so that Cazetti could see it under the light. "'Radio Battalion intercept: Unidentified voice on tactical net. Secure. Vicinity Alayah. Interrogative *Hitman* Interrogative *Cazetti*. Affirmative *Pacifico—Pacifico*. Break transmission.' . . . What the hell is this?"

"The convent in Alayah has a radio, sir."

"How did they come up on the tactical net secure?"

"The radio is one of ours."

"How did they get it?"

"I gave it to them, sir. It was an old one."

"Oh! An old one! You think, then, that's okay? With crypto-gear? Are you insane? In Alayah! When?"

"When the Gunner got married up there."

"What did you do that for?"

"It was so they could call for help if they needed it. And sir, I think they're in bad trouble."

"Every goddamn body in the Root is in bad trouble, Cazetti. Especially you. We're in a *battle*. Did you notice that today?"

"I noticed, sir."

"We weren't sent here to protect a bunch of goddamn nuns, you know."

"Why were we sent, sir?"

"I don't goddamn know. But on account of you, there's crypto-gear in unknown hands, my tactical net is penetrated, and this is serious." Captain Mac snapped his glasses off and lit a cigarette and began to think with his head pinched in his hand. "Those nuns are in a convent or a monastery or something like that."

"Yes, sir."

"You've been there. It's got a high wall, right?"

"Yes, sir. Real high."

"That's why I can't get a muzzle flash on those goddamn guns. They're behind the convent wall."

"Sir, you can't fire the grid. There's nuns in it."

"The Navy blew an orphanage to hell about ten minutes ago. I think I can do what I want."

"Sir, anyway, don't."

"Those guns have killed at Bravo Company, and I'm going to fire the grid. The colonel is right there and he wants that grid. He might want you for treason too. That depends on how I feel after we hang fire on the convent, heavy. Then you get out of here. You get down on the line and you stay there until relieved, notified, or killed. Is that clear?"

Captain Mac stood up. He shouted. "Colonel,

Cazetti turned a grid on those tubes in Alayah. It's a fortified poz. Request seventy-five rounds of five-inch Naval guns."

"Permission granted. Repeat if necessary."

"Stand up, Cazetti. Give the colonel the grid."

Cazetti stood and stared at Captain Mac. To the colonel he said, "Four-four-one, four-one-one."

The Fire Support Coordinator radioed the Navy. Cazetti geared up. He bolted out the entry of the COC. He crouched by the fallen palm trees and looked out at the range. The Naval guns fired five minutes later, long and heavy in the semi-dark. Cazetti could hear the rounds scump out from the ships, and he could see the impact in Alayah and then he could hear the rumble of the rounds come back from the range. The impacts in Alayah flashed and sparkled awesomely. The sound drifted back in a low stewing-boil of thunder. There was an agony to the thing.

When there was a lull, he got a ride at the Battalion inside a Trac to look for Corporal Paugh on the line. He found him at Whiskey-Six on the perimeter.

Whiskey-Six was a Bravo Company hooch with flaws. It stood to the south of other hooches on the perimeter. It was small, it was not stout. A sign hung on it: "PAYBACK IS A MEDEVAC." It rose from the sand around it, a caved-in square chunk with a skirt of sandbag wall. The sea was close at hand.

A month of heavy fire had made Paugh, Doc Latour, and Lieutenant Irish dazed. Cazetti was troubled by their look. They looked gone. Some regular thing inside them was missing. They sat with their backs against the hooch, staring, and lifting up the finger over the sandbags to the snipers. There was no shelter from the sun or rain except within the sagging square center of the hooch which they called the Inner Sanctum. The Inner Sanctum was not big enough to lie down in. A radio played and a wind carried it out to the surf.

"Check it out, man. This is Whiskey-Six," Doc said. "You'll like it here. We sing 'Oh Tannenbaum' and we got porno from the Red Cross pallet. Definitely, we got cocoa saved up and tons of 203-grenades. We dig. We burn some bandoleers for real. You'll like it, Cazetti."

"That's enough, Doc," the lieutenant said.

Cazetti didn't like it.

"So. You're on charges?" Lieutenant Irish asked.

"That's probably so, sir."

"Don't you love Beirut?"

Paugh was looking out with binoculars. A mortar came in suckling, Paugh looked out. He didn't duck. On the impact, shrapnel came chung-ing overhead. A giant moth landed on the lieutenant's boot. He shot it with his pistol.

"Eew," said the lieutenant.

"I got some Druze moving in that building," Paugh said. It was a flat square building with holes knocked out of it. "Get some now, Cazetti."

"Well, all right," the lieutenant said. "Let's fire it."

They were smearing bolts with lubricant.

"Let's do fire, from the rear, huh!" said Doc.

They were pressing magazines with speed loaders.

"Let's go, you commie tool-hangers," said Paugh.

Doc and Paugh crawled out with a machine gun and set it in a divot of a grassy bank. The lieutenant gave the signal. They opened up the gun. The lieutenant started popping the 203-grenade rounds into the building. Cazetti salted the windows with his rifle. A rocketed grenade took off from an upstairs window. It hit between the divot and the hooch. It did not hurt the hooch, but stunned it, and Doc and Paugh yelled out they were okay, they were okay, but the grass around their flank caught fire. The Druze's small-arms waved out horizontal lines of rounds. The tops of sandbags split. Rounds did a zizzing past Cazetti's ear. A gasping fear took hold of him. The lieutenant was yelling, but Cazetti couldn't hear the words. The thinned and blurry sights on the handle on the rifle jolted at his eye. The inside workings of the rifle, recoiling and machining rounds, pinned his concentration to a jerking dot of light. The Druze were moving between the blasted holes and falling back to a wire-wrung berm. Then the smoke from the burning grass blew across the field of view. Another rocketed grenade came in and hit the forward skirt of the sandbag wall. It knocked the lieutenant and Cazetti down. Cazetti's head was buzzing, prickly, his mouth tasted of metal. He saw the lieutenant grab his forehead and his glasses fell to the ground. He yelled. He stood again. Cazetti imitated him. He set the rifle on the parapet and fired out. He did not look. The other hooches in the area started firing. A Trac came down the perimeter road and let out its big machine gun. Then it was quiet.

Paugh and Doc came back. They were sweating. Paugh left the machine gun on its legs with the butt sitting up on an ammo can. Doc lay down and dropped his head on a carton of C-rats.

"Check it out, man. This is Whiskey-Six."

Cazetti lay down in the sand between the skirt of sandbags and the Inner Sanctum. He left his cheek in the sand and looked over the sand. A can was stuck into the sand. It seemed to be a can of beef. Cazetti was too tired to ascertain the truth of it. He stared at the can. He was too tired to open his eyes, or close them.

"I am here," he thought. "I am nothing here. Am I anywhere? I am not something. I am no one. In a skin. There is nowhere else. But alive."

"Are you being stupid?"

He smiled.

It was dark. Paugh kept looking out with night-vision goggles and ducking down, and standing up. A Lebanese panhard fired down an alley cluttered with metal junk. The sound of ricochets was a clanging, tearing demon. Artillery came in to the north of Whiskey-Six, sending up the white drifting genie pillars of phosphorous.

Doc sang "Oh Tannenbaum." It was day and mortars came in and Cazetti hunched with Doc inside the Inner Sanctum. It was night and there was another firefight and Whiskey-Six shot out. And when they were sleeping, Armor-Piercing-

Incendiary-Tracers from a .50-cal fired down into the hooch from the hills, and the tracer rounds hit down from above in a way from which there was no cover. The rounds hit into the hooch and sparked madly. They called in mortars to knock out the big machine gun. The mortars had trouble doing it. They put their heads onto the sand, and pressed the sand with their heads and had no cover. They got sand in their mouths yelling into it.

The range was lit by illumination rounds and the burning towns. The Navy fired long and heavy into Alayah.

"They hammer on that town," Lieutenant Irish said.

"There's a mechanized column trying to come down the road up there," Cazetti said. "There's a lot of tanks. I know a guy up there. He's a Christian Leb. Joe Sfir."

"I bet you *used to* know him," Lieutenant Irish said. "I bet he *used to* be a Leb. If he's still in Alayah, he's probably a corpse."

When morning came, the USS *New Jersey* came, driving north along the coast with its big guns pointing in-country. The city looked at it in awe, and for a short time there was a vacant hush of peace.

Cain and Minovich and Davey were coming in a jeep, rushing down the undulated road toward Whiskey-Six. They saw Corporal Paugh and the lieutenant sitting by the machine gun with its chamber latch cocked up.

"You got our duty-flick in there?" Cain asked.

"He's inside. He's resting. Ain't he resting?" said Paugh.

The lieutenant nodded and looked over the water at the *New Jersey*. He called Cazetti out. Cazetti crawled out of the hooch. He stayed lying on his stomach.

"Come on," said Minovich.

"What for?" Cazetti asked.

"You got a mission."

"A mission? No. My court-martial is coming through. I'm going to the brig."

"Now, don't look at going to jail, bud," Davey said. "That radio turned out okay."

"It's a real-life photo mission," said Minovich.

"I'm not enticed. I'm angry. I'm mad at the whole thing. They dropped a couple hundred rounds of Naval gun on that place."

"Yeah, they did," Minovich said. "But that's all right. It didn't hurt your nun. Joe Sfir and Hitman trucked them out and got them into Junieh."

"You're lying to me, and your lie is dumb."

"Think what you want to, bud. You're getting in this jeep. When you get up to Alpha Company you can talk to Hitman and he'll tell you all about it." Davey pinched his forelock up. "Remember what I told you about the Suck, bud? I don't lie to you."

"Gentlemen," said Minovich. "We're taking back our duty-flick."

"I thank you for the loan," Lieutenant Irish said. "We burned some bandoleers together."

Cain wiggled the gearshift knob. "Cazetti. Get in the jeep."

Cazetti stood and gathered up his gear, "What's this for again?"

Davey answered him. "You're going up to Alpha Company on a resupply convoy. Get photos of the hostile bunkers. We're going to knock them out with fixed-wing air."

They left Cazetti off outside the great Battalion Headquarters building in front of the shower tents. There were some wounded being attended outside of the Aide Station. The convoy was a dozen trucks. Some had big machine guns mounted on turrets over the cabs. Cazetti screwed together the long-range recon camera, which they had brought along in the jeep. He walked down the row of trucks until he found the one Yoches was driving.

"I want your Six-by," Cazetti said, looking up at Yoches. "Have you got room?"

"Can do," said Yoches. The chinstrap of his helmet shook off from the side.

"Make sure you get me home."

Yoches said, "You picked the Cadillac of Six-by's, Cazetti. Yoches gets you there and I always got room for one more."

Cazetti kicked up into the back. The convoy plowed out from Battalion.

Alpha Company was cut off from the lines at the distance of a mile, as the crow would fly. It was stuck out at a University building on the Sidon road. To get to it, the convoy had to loop around the city, taking roads under the control of vaguely friendly forces. The trucks bounced in the rubble and the craters on the roads. The gunners traced along windows with the turreted machine guns, or leveled them on pedestrians that were glaring at the trucks. The city thronged with traffic, and stray incidents of fire occurred on the flanks of the route, the city filled with faces, horns, rattling, mobs.

The clouds stood in piles over the water, hanging over the *New Jersey*. Rain was coming from the sea. The grunts at Alpha Company had a more retarded stare than the stare at Whiskey-Six. They were blown with a torpid, dripping blankness. They looked dumb. A working party unhitched their harnesses and began unloading the Six-By's. Radio blurbs and hisses came from the cabs of the trucks. The building they were using was scorched and blown. It was abandoned and the grunts stayed down in a concrete moat, and in hooches and trenches lined with sandbags where the ground tumbled away from the building.

Cazetti was looking for Spyglass, the observation post on the roof where Ballory the sniper worked. He climbed a stairway up, and then a ladder to the roof. He came out at a square sandbagged turret. Ballory was lying down with his Winchester on his chest. To his right there was a pool of sticky blood, and a viscera of mossy tufts, where hair was stuck. There was a trench periscope on a tripod, binoculars hanging from it, and the radio hissed. The wind blew.

"Long time," Ballory said. They shook hands.

"The COC wants photos of the bunkers that keep hitting you. They're going to bring in fixed-wing and knock them out."

"This command has geniuses, I swear. That's a military idea, to kill what's trying to kill you. Hey, not bad."

Cazetti pointed to the mess he saw. "Somebody caught a round?"

"Yeah, man," Ballory said, "It was a shame. It really was." He heaved a sigh. "Last night we were taking mortars and my partner bought some shrapnel. Today a damn major came up to spot for me. Seven-six-two in the head. I tell you, man, that major changed my whole idea about rank."

"Well, it was quick," Cazetti said.

"Very quick. I know."

"Show me the bunkers."

Ballory stood and pointed. "They dig for a while, shoot for a while, then go to the Cafe Danielle for hash and coffee. You see the cafe? Tell them to hit it." Cazetti took a picture of a red building with an awning at the base. "The terrace of that building with the Amal flag on it. They open up from there. There's recoilless rifles underground that come out of that culvert where the road turns. I don't like that. Tell them to hit it."

They came below to the open floor at the base of the building where the moat was, with its parapet of sandbags. The grunts were eating cookies and cramming rounds in magazines, dazing off at the Hooterville. Ballory pointed at the figures of kafiyah-wrapped gunmen standing with an anti-aircraft gun between two hovels sprouting ears of naked rebar.

It was beginning to rain. Ponchos came on in the moat. It was a cold gray rain. Ballory looked through it at the ships. He had to kick up on the balls of his feet to see over the parapet.

"How'd you like to be on ship right now?"

"I don't think of that no more," said Ballory.

"Me neither."

"Our guys at the posts out there, 69 and 35, man, it's bad for them. We resupplied them with an ice-cream truck, but they've been cut off too long. They get rolled up with anti-aircraft guns, and I don't know. What do you know? Are they getting out?"

"How would I know?"

"You're with Intell. You're supposed to know."

"Sorry," Cazetti said. "I don't know."

A black lance-corporal with a set of radios stood up on his knees. "Captain Hill, sir. Valuable says to expect some fire anytime."

The captain, with binoculars, looked out from the moat. "What kind?"

"Most kinds. And snipe, sir."

"Get the convoy out."

Along the moat the bolts went home.

"You want to stay for this one, Cazetti?" Ballory asked.

"No," Cazetti said. "Ballory, I'm looking for a guy. Hitman Hitchins. He was here, they told me. Is he still here?"

"Ain't he a major?"

"Yeah. You know where he is? Is he still here?"

"Just the part you saw upstairs. And the part that's going out on truck. Sorry, man."

The trucks were turning over. Cazetti was stunned. Ballory walked him out to the trucks.

"Go, man. Go on," Ballory said. Rain was spattering.

Cazetti kicked up from the tire. The body was wrapped up in a poncho and the rain spattered on the poncho. The stiff feet in boots stuck out. Ballory reached over the slat-sides of the Six-by to shake hands with Cazetti.

"Sorry. He was a good man. Quick. You know."

The trucks pulled out in the rain. They took the same looping route through the city in the gloomy gray light with the crowds, the tension, the traffic. The truck bounced, the body shook and slid around in the bed of the truck, and Cazetti looked out at the faces and the rain and the guns while the Six-by's went smoking through the city.

Yoches pulled his Six-by out of convoy and took it down to a runway on the shore side of the terminal building at the airport. There was a two-rotor chopper with its tailgate down and a crew chief standing in back of it, coiling the comm-wire to his cranial. The colonel stood by there at his jeep with Neale and Mangas. Cazetti handed the body down to Neale and Mangas, then the three of them ran it under the rotor-wash into the bird with the poncho flapping wildly.

They pulled back from the bird and stood with the colonel. The bird took off and the colonel saluted it, and Neale and Mangas and Cazetti saluted it too.

They got aboard the colonel's jeep. Fire popped up around a checkpoint bunker on the airport road.

The colonel spoke to Neale. "Slide along the terminal."

Neale pulled around the terminal traffic circle, which was mobbed with a hustle of frantic passengers trying to get out on a waiting PanAm jet. Neale pressed the jeep through. Cazetti looked across the crowd. His eye picked up a few asprin-shaped crowns in the mob.

"Stop! Neale!"

"We're not stopping," the colonel said.

"Let me out. I'll meet you at the COC."

Neale snapped his head around to Cazetti. "I can't stop so sit down, man!"

"I'll meet you at the COC. I'll be all right."

"Sit yourself down," the colonel said.

Mangas tentatively held onto Cazetti by the cargo pouch on his trousers.

"I'll be five minutes!" Cazetti jumped out of the jeep. He ran into the crowd and pushed himself into it. Neale stopped the jeep at the fringe of the crowds near the wall that led to the perimeter. In the jeep they looked around for Cazetti but he had been swallowed into the stream.

Cazetti jerked through the crowd. He saw the old nun's face and the old nun saw him. In a tender way, she smiled, and then she touched her forehead with her wrist. The crowd made a terrible cacophony of guttural Arabic shouting, and bodies were being pressed. A barrier of bodies formed between Cazetti and the old nun. He could spot more nuns behind her. There were bright fluorescent lights and crammed baggage wrapped with duct tape. Babies wailed. There was a rustle of plastic bags. Cazetti pushed through.

Finally he reached the old nun.

"Where is Philomena?" he shouted.

"I am very obliged to you," the old nun said. "I would not have believed it." She was calm, and that irked Cazetti.

"You owe me nothing. You owe the major who came for you. He is dead."

"Nevertheless, I am obliged. I will certainly pray for that major."

"I don't care. Where is Philomena? That's all I want to know."

"She is, well, I prefer not to tell you. Please wait."

"No!" Cazetti shouted. "I cannot wait. You tell me now."

"There is no reason to say it. Please wait. Please, you tire me."

"I'm in a hurry. Do you understand that?" Cazetti shouted. He was agonized and feared he would cry. "Where is Philomena? Just *tell* me."

"I am also in a hurry," the old nun said. "She is there." She moved her head. Cazetti looked.

He saw her coming from the door of the WC. There were many heads between them, and the view he had of her was cut by the moving crowd. He saw her nose pointing around a little, then he did not see her. She was pressing through in his direction. Her cowl was down on her shoulders. He pressed towards her. When he got near her, she caught him squarely in her eyes. She stared at first, then slapped her hands up to her face covering everything but her nose.

Mangas and Neale came through the press of people. They were angry and they grabbed Cazetti by the war-belt. "Get out. Get out. Come on."

"Let go!" Cazetti shouted.

Cazetti broke loose and pressed toward Philomena again. He could see her. She let her hands down, tears shimmered in her eyes, and her nose pointed in a pitiful way.

Cazetti got close to her. She tossed him the *dizanier* off her thumb. He did not catch it, and it fell onto the floor. It got kicked around by the shuffling feet. Cazetti dropped to his knees to snatch it up. Mangas and Neale caught him up by the harness again. They yanked on him, and got him to his feet.

"Get in the jeep."

"Get your hands off," Cazetti said.

"The colonel is outside, man!"

"I don't care."

"Cazetti. Knock it off."

He looked. He lost sight of her. Mangas and Neale pulled him along by the harness straps.

"Goddamn let me go!" Cazetti said. The

dizanier fell out of his hand while he was trying to shake out of the flak jacket and the harness. The flak jacket came off in Mangas's hand. Cazetti dropped down to reach for the *dizanier*. It lay at the base of an ashtray. He got it in his fingers. Mangas and Neale yanked him up again.

"This isn't funny, my friend."

"I'm not making a joke. Let go."

"You're getting in the jeep." Neale and Mangas pulled him to the foyer where the colonel was standing peering over the crowd.

The colonel was angry. "Get him out of there!"

When they got Cazetti to the colonel, the colonel stuck his finger in Cazetti's neck. "Are you trying to bother me some more?"

"No, sir. It was the people Hitman trucked out of Alayah with Joe Sfir. I wanted to say good-bye."

"Get in the jeep," the colonel said. He was easier. "We thought you were trying to get on a plane."

"I wish I thought of that, sir," Cazetti said as he climbed into the jeep.

They pulled into the jeep park in front of the COC. The colonel walked in directly. Cazetti climbed a ladder to the roof of the COC. He waited there. He was humming "Wonderful

Dream." It sounded bassy. It sounded good bassy. Tracers began to fly across the hillsides. In time, the PanAm jet pulled up off the runway. It flew out over the ships, over the water. It became a light blinking in the rain clouds. It disappeared.

He was wet when he walked back into the COC. It was lit with the old yellow cast the rain weather gave to it. The Lebanese oil heater had appeared again, with cans and canteens on it. The rains were beating for the second time. Cazetti pulled a canteen cup and drew coffee from a bull. He went back in to the partition of the -2 and he undid his gear. He sat down and he was tired.

"Did you get the photos?" asked Captain Mac. His tone was kind. It troubled Cazetti.

"Yeah," he said.

"The fact is, we don't need them anymore. We're pulling Alpha Company and the checkpoints into the perimeter."

"Oh, well . . ." Cazetti said. He looked at the little cross and the loop of wooden beads in his hand.

"Joe Sfir made it out of Alayah, bud. Did you hear that?" Davey asked.

"What a big thrill."

"He got lucky," Garces said.

"He bought his luck," Cain said.

"You can't buy luck. That's ridiculous," Garces said. "In any case, there's providence as well as luck. There's steering with your indicators too."

"This conversation bugs me," Cain said. "We are pretty well screwed, Garces, and you know it. Look at your map."

"Cain, don't talk that talk," said Captain Mac.

"I don't care, sir. It's true."

"We're getting out of here. That's imperative. That's absolute."

"I didn't come ashore the day before yesterday."

"Shut up, Cain," Davey said.

Cazetti curled the *dizanier* in his fist and looked away. It was not long he looked. Artillery came in again. The COC cranked up.

Pale light came in through chipped-out vent holes in the cellar where Cazetti was lying on his cot, listening to the fire out in the Hooterville, out on the line, up on the range. He was bored. The fire bored him. His bones were sore and stiff. He was tired of going topside and dealing with guns. He had a fever and his joints ached. His eyes hurt. When he moved them he saw Mangas asleep next to Cicchelero. His head poked out of a poncho liner. He looked at Neale. Neale was asleep. He wanted to sleep but he ached and felt bored of trying to sleep, and aching.

"I'm going to give birth to you. Yes. That's it."

He did not conjure up her voice, but it came inside his head, with her hands trembling around. "I'm Philomena . . . I am very *feconde,* you see . . ."

"Let go! . . ." His own voice visited him, he was visiting himself, struggling against his harness straps. "Goddamn let me go! . . ." he muttered. "Let go. Don't do like that. Let go."

The bodies in the cots lifted up from the cots into the air. He saw them. He saw his own body was in the air. They crashed to the floor with sounds of heaping metal and concrete tons falling in. A rush of smoke was sucked into the cellar. A chaotic wave of shouting rose. Zippo lighters flared and made infernal orange light in the smoke. Gear was scrambled and there were choked-out coughs.

"Any wounded? Any wounded?"

"Are you okay?"

"Get your gear on. Mount out of here. Saddle up!"

They coughed and got their gear on and tugged each other up the stairwell, rising.

They came out to ground feeling it with their feet, making sure of it. It was a very sunny day. They were tapping magazines on the helmets and locking up the rifles on some pointless kind of assault. The sky was blue. They could see a giant cloud of black smoke with churls of white dust rising from where the three hundred men at the Battalion had been. They crossed a sea of rubble, they crossed a hedgerow stripped of all its leaves, which fell and made a fine green coverlet on the ground. They walked into the cloud. It swallowed them, man by man. It was darkening and brightening, lingering, pouring up, and for a moment the rattle of the fire in the Hooterville was stopped.

They came out at the site of the blast, a carnage heap of agony in the shape of a giant bowl of cereal overturned. Black sweeps of shadow spiked the glaring white gray mangles of concrete. The rubble thickened where they went. It got deeper. Bloody severed limbs appeared. The pieces of body were bigger here and there. On the limbs of certain trees, bodies hung up, speared, and blood was dripping. A powder-coated grunt was carried on a stretcher like a screaming floured chicken leg. His side was opened to the hip, revealing the innards of the abdomen. His penis hung by one flap of scrotum. Where they walked around the smoking heap of rubble, touching ground, the blood mixed with the earth and formed a mud that oozed around the boot soles, clogging them. At the higher sections of the heap were sleeping bags, dangling and dripping blood from the weighted end like coffee filters. The sweet concrete dust and blood death smell clung to the nose.

There was gas inside the crushed, in-caved pockets of the building where Cazetti crawled, and kneeled, and pulled on parts of blocks of wall, and parts of men, and there was screaming there, and dripping blood. Cazetti crawled around in there. His eyes hurt and his bones ached. A shot rang out inside the heap. He crawled to the sound of the shot. The man who shot himself could not be pulled. Cazetti crawled out and climbed up the outside of the heap.

Garces was conscious. His shoulders rose above the rubble. Two rods of rebar had pronged him through the middle like the tines of a fork. Where they came out in front, he held the rebar firm. He said he was okay. He said he was okay again. He died there, like that, clinging to the rebar.

Cazetti climbed down and he met Mangas in the rubble hills around the heap. Mangas held his face. Tears made a crust of the powder coating it. He was pale with the clinging dust, his hair powdered gray with it.

"My life. My whole life . . ."

They saw a body there, where they were standing. They put it on a stretcher where it landed facing down. The face had eyes that were whole, and blue, moist and clear, they were popped out and hanging on the optical cord.

"He looks too dumb," Cazetti said. He slid out his bayonet. His eyes hurt and his joints ached.

"No, Cazetti. Don't!"

"He looks too dumb."

Cazetti grabbed the eye cords together. He cut them. He threw the eyes away. They took the stretcher to a Six-by parked behind the blasted hedge. It was heaped high with corpses. The tailgate was down. Blood was dripping through the tailgate hinge.

There was room for one more, so they took the body and swung it and tossed it partway up the heap. It made a quiver in the heap. The Six-by pulled away. Another one backed in, empty, smeared with blood. For a short time, snipers fired, and Mangas and Cazetti took cover in the rubble. Then the snipers were killed.

They went back into the heaps, and did some E-tool digging, pulling around the clacking rubble chunks, digging without speaking, stiffened from the tingle of the death surrounding them. Big equipment suddenly arrived on site. Cranes and bulldozers made the sounds of a junkyard in the gory twisted paroxysm. Cazetti saw a crane driver talk into a handset and drop the bucket of the crane with a smile. In the rubble then, Cazetti found Cain's body; burly, naked, dried by powder dust. Cain was in two pieces. Next to him, there was a naked female back. Cazetti and Mangas rolled it over. The mouth was crushed with rubble. The dead eyes leaked bright blood from behind.

They pulled her out with Cain. She seemed to have no muscles. She was only soft-wrapped bones. She tumbled in the bed of the Six-by languidly. The sergeant-major screamed. He looked to be a shadow in the haze of the angled sun. He was screaming for a corpsman. The corpsman was screaming that he had no shots of morphine.

Neale had a captain on his lap who needed morphine. Neale was very tender. He stroked the captain until he died. Then he wandered up to Mangas and Cazetti near the trucks, and in a moment, crazed and bitter, tried to climb up into one of them. Mangas yanked him off. Neale got mad at him. They threw punches at each other, but they stopped.

There was a screech of wind. Shrapnel stung into the trucks. Mangas and Neale ran diving for a hooch, but Cazetti didn't move. He heard Minovich and Davey shouting from a roof above the trucks, where there was a big machine gun firing out across the airport road. Cazetti tried to shout to them, shouting and pointing at the cranes, repeating his motion with his mouth stuck open, like a mechanical man popped out of a clock. Davey heard him shouting and shouted back at him. He jerked his thumb hard over his shoulder, directed at the hooch. Cazetti made a leap to ditch himself in the hooch where Neale and Mangas were, then stopped. He turned. He took the rifle off his back, locked it up with rounds, and started firing on a crane. He was kneeling, shooting up a crane when he was thrown backward by a mortar that came in. When it hit, he shook the shake he felt. His back snapped hard against the ground and a shriek tore out of him.

The operators of the cranes were taken prisoner after that, after making radio transmissions from the cabs of the cranes, which were taken in by intercept, calling mortars in and sending out descriptions of their victory. They were taken to the Ice House in a hurry.

A Six-by idled at LZ Rock where Minovich and Davey stood around, scowling and spitting with their hands on their hips and their heads bent down. The weather had turned gloomy. A bird dropped down with the rain in the lull and waited for the load. It had a military number. The bird lifted up, spinning the blackened vortex of the rain in the rotors, and it nosed over the tarmac, the beach and the waves, getting little as it moved offshore.

Artillery came in, and rains came in from the sea. The air was filled with the blue rain and rotors. The LZ was piled with bloody cots and aluminum coffins. No one slept. No one was hungry. Heavy missiles and an overrun were expected. The perimeter got hit from the Hooterville. The Battery fired out. The Navy sent the fixed-wing air. The *New Jersey* laid its guns out on the range.

They waited in the hooches, hunched in the womb of the earth, looking over the sandbags with the grim stuck-eye, while Time brought up the wind, and the wind hummed a song along the wires. The few autumn leaves there stuck on the blades of the wire; a few came blowing into the hooches.

In time, the survivors there were rotated out, were ferried to homebound ships. The sound of fire disappeared. The hush on the sea was inscrutable. The horizon closed over the city and the range. Through the backs of their eyes it was sinking into nothing like their thoughts in the staring silences. The hum inside the ship and the valve-sucked air supplies stuffed the mind with an ether. It was quiet going home.

Mangas crossed a red-lit cargo hold, ducking his head again and again under the barrels of the lined, shackled, and silent artillery. He climbed up a ladder. He opened up a hatch. Neale was sitting along a breezeway with his back against a bulkhead. It was a bright, windy day. He was looking out at the twinkling sea, squinting at the flares of shimmer on the water, and the gush of the blue and the white. They traded a tired and a vanquished look, then tightened up their squints. Mangas pulled out of his pocket the little wooden beads and cross the nun had tossed to Cazetti, and he asked Neale if he knew what kin to send them to. Neale said he didn't know, but figured there should be a name somewhere in Cazetti's file in the brig, and they could go down there and talk to Cossaboom. Mangas didn't want to; neither did Neale. It didn't seem what they should do. They said it was the customary thing to commend it to the deep. They commended it. They saw it carry on the water into the wake stretched out to the east, and they stayed together there with their backs against the bulkhead, looking for a time at the sea.

REVERGE ANSELMO was born in Mexico City in 1962. He served three years in the U.S. Marine Corps and is a survivor of the Expedition sent to Lebanon. He graduated from the Erv Malnarich Outfitters and Guides School in Hamilton, Montana, and attended St. John's College in Santa Fe, New Mexico. He lived for many years in Paris and was a businessman in Europe and Latin America. He is the son of the late Rene Anselmo, the communications tycoon.

The Cadillac of Six-by's is his first novel.